"I'm sorry, Hallie. The last thing I want to do is offend you. I want to close the door on that chapter of my life forever."

"I don't blame you."

"But will you be able to forgive me?"

She jerked her head around. He saw a blur of blue-green fire. "How can you ask me that? Don't you realize I'm your friend?"

Friend.

In his gut he recognized he wanted her to be more than that to him....

Rebecca Winters, an American writer and mother of four, is excited to be in this new millennium because it means another new beginning. Having said goodbye to the classroom where she taught French and Spanish, she is now free to spend more time with her family, to travel and to write the Harlequin Romance® novels she loves so dearly.

Rebecca loves to hear from readers. If you wish to e-mail her, please visit her Web site at: www.rebeccawinters-author.com.

Books by Rebecca Winters

THE FRENCHMAN'S BRIDE

Rebecca Winters

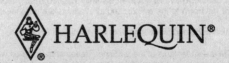

TORONTO • NEW YORK • LONDON
AMSTERDAM • PARIS • SYDNEY • HAMBURG
STOCKHOLM • ATHENS • TOKYO • MILAN • MADRID
PRAGUE • WARSAW • BUDAPEST • AUCKLAND

ISBN 0-373-03779-1

THE FRENCHMAN'S BRIDE

First North American Publication 2004.

Copyright © 2003 by Rebecca Winters.

This edition published by arrangement with Harlequin Books S.A.

Visit us at www.eHarlequin.com

Printed in U.S.A.

CHAPTER ONE

REACHING for a towel, Vincent Rolland stepped from the shower of his London hotel suite having made the decision to fly to Paris after his business lunch later in the day. This weekend he'd be taking his twins home to St. Genes. He couldn't wait.

The chateau had been like a tomb without them. Though there'd been phone calls and visits, the nine month school year had been too long a separation.

It was Thursday. They weren't expecting him until Friday, but he wanted to surprise them. Tonight they would celebrate the end of school together before flying home to their chateau tomorrow.

While he was shaving, he heard his cell phone ring. It was probably one of the children calling him now.

He hurried into the other room to answer it. A glance at the caller ID told him someone from St. Genes was ringing.

Hopefully nothing was wrong.

"Oui?"

"Bonjour, Vincent." It was the housekeeper. She sounded in good spirits.

"Bonjour, Etvige. How's Pere Maurice?"

"Don't worry. He and Beauregard just left on their morning walk."

That was reassuring; with the twins away, his grandfather and the dog were becoming devoted to each other.

"Monsieur Gide at the bank in Paris called you. He'd

like you to phone him as soon as you can. Here's his number."

Monsieur Gide? Vincent hadn't talked to him since he'd set up an account for the twins last fall.

He wrote it down. "*Merci*, Etvige. Tell Pere Maurice I'll call him from Paris."

Once they'd hung up, he punched in the number and was put through to the bank manager.

"Thank you for getting back to me so quickly, Monsieur Rolland. You did say to phone if the need arose."

"Of course. What can I do for you?"

"I wanted to let you know that two days ago your son wrote a check for a large sum of money. Before I put it through, I thought I should call to be certain you approved."

"How large?"

"Eighty-seven hundred Eurodollars. There'll be nothing left in the account."

On hearing the banker's words, disappointment swept through Vincent that his children hadn't waited for him before they spent it.

"It's all right, Monsieur. I promised them a car if they did well in their end of year exams."

"A car? I'm afraid this check was made out to Rue Vendome Fine Jewelry."

Jewelry—

A shudder passed through his body.

Just hearing the word was like an echo from the blackest period of his life.

"Hold the check until I've made an inquiry."

"Very good, Monsieur. Here's the number."

As soon as Vincent hung up, he called the jewelry store.

Vincent couldn't imagine what this was all about. On the whole his children had always exercised good judgment and were trustwor—

"Bijoux Vendome."

"Bonjour, Monsieur. I'd like to talk to the manager please."

"Speaking."

"This is Vincent Rolland."

"Oh yes, Monsieur Rolland. Just the other day your son was in to buy an exquisite ring for the woman he intends to marry. He is very much in love and insisted on the finest aquamarine to match her eyes."

"Mon Dieu," Vincent whispered in agony.

He gripped the phone tighter. History was repeating itself. Like father, like son...

"Hallie?"

Hallie Linn had just left Tati's department store in Paris where she worked when she heard a familiar voice. She glanced to her left. A taxi had pulled up alongside her and the rear door was flung open.

In the back sat Monique Rolland, the vivacious French girl who'd attached herself to Hallie over the last school year.

"What are you doing here?"

"Waiting for you. It's your birthday! We're going to celebrate!"

Birthday? She'd completely forgotten about it.

Furthermore, Hallie had already said a final goodbye to Monique and her brother Paul two days ago. Hallie was sure that this was just another excuse to get the three of them together before the twins went home to the Dordogne region of France for the summer.

Monique's unexpected presence outside Hallie's

work meant the motherless teen still couldn't let go and was feeling the wrench of separation.

In truth, so was Hallie.

While she'd been in Paris doing service as a lay nun for the Dominican's international outreach program, she'd learned to love the precocious twins like family. To spend any more time with them would make it that much harder for Hallie to leave. But she had to; Hallie would be entering a convent in San Diego, California, in two weeks.

"How did you know it was my birthday? I didn't even remember it."

"When we crossed the Channel to spend the day in England Paul sneaked a peek at your passport. Now get in the taxi!" she cried. "We're blocking the traffic!"

Hallie didn't budge. "You're supposed to be at school right now. You know very well they're having a farewell dinner for everyone."

"I'd rather be with you. Don't worry. I obtained special permission to stay out until eight o'clock. Come on. We're wasting time."

At this point the impatient taxi driver muttered a curse, prompting Hallie into action. Against her better judgment she climbed in the back seat. Once she'd shut the door, the driver darted into the crush of traffic. It was a miracle they didn't have an accident.

"Where are we going exactly?"

Monique flashed her a mischievous smile. "That's my surprise."

"Another one?"

There'd been so many throughout the last nine months, but Monique had never shown up in a taxi before. They normally walked or took the subway and trains.

"Is it far?"

There was a hint of mystery in Monique's expression. "Wait and see."

"Look me in the eye and swear that your headmistress said you could stay out late."

With a toss of her head, Monique dismissed Hallie's concerns as utter nonsense.

"I thought so," Hallie murmured. "Not only are you breaking the rules, if we travel much further, this taxi ride is going to cost too much money for your budget. I'm getting out at the next intersection."

"No!" Monique cried out. "You can't do that or you'll spoil everything!"

A certain nuance in Monique's voice told her that not only had the twins organized something elaborate, they'd been planning it for a long time.

"You know I don't want to ruin your surprise, but I'd hate to see either of you get into trouble on your last school night."

"I passed my finals with highest marks. Besides, the headmistress wouldn't dare get me into trouble with Papa."

"Why not?"

"Because he never forgets to bring her a supply of the best wine from our vineyards when he comes to Paris." Her dark brows arched. "She wouldn't want that to end, or the visits. So far he has resisted her attempts to seduce him, but she hasn't given up yet."

The cynical comment coming from the mouth of such a wonderful young woman wounded Hallie.

"Don't look so shocked, I've told you before that all women find my father irresistible, money or not."

While Hallie was digesting this latest confidence about the headmistress, she noticed they had arrived in the sixteenth arrondissement, an area noted for being one of the most prestigious residential neighborhoods in Paris.

The taxi drove along the Rue de Passy with its many shops, then turned down another road and eventually pulled up in front of an apartment building. It was a beautiful example of Fin de Siècle architecture. Only the extremely wealthy, like Monique's father, could afford to live here.

Hallie followed Monique out of the taxi. Once she'd paid the driver, they entered the elegant lobby where she punched in a code so they could ride the elevator.

It took them to the third floor where the doors opened to an exquisite apartment with expansive rooms. Much of the furniture and fixtures were fine antiques, yet the sumptuous appointments created a welcoming feel.

Monique walked over to the French doors which led to a terrace. "Wow!" She darted Hallie a gamin smile. "Your own private view of the Bois de Boulogne."

Paris in the spring. It was a glorious sight, but Hallie couldn't concentrate on the view when she had serious reservations about spending more time with the twins.

"Does your father know about this?"

"Oh la la! For your information he's in London on business and won't come for us until tomorrow afternoon. Paul and I have been given permission to use the apartment for special occasions. Your twenty-fifth birthday is just such an event."

Though Hallie had never met Vincent Rolland, she secretly admired him. For a single parent he seemed to have done an excellent job of raising his children. They didn't smoke, take drugs or abuse alcohol. Both were exceptional students, bright and charming. In Hallie's

opinion they were quite outstanding. He deserved a
great deal of credit for being a terrific father.

What she couldn't understand was why he'd sent
them away to boarding school. How had he stood to be
parted from them? As for the twins, they adored him.
Hallie knew they lived for his visits and telephone calls.

"I'd hate to think you were taking advantage of your
father's generosity because of me."

"Of course we're not! As I've told you before, you
worry about us too much. We'll only be here for an
hour. *S'il te plait,* don't be a, how do you say it? Wet
rug?" She stamped her well shod foot, impatient for
Hallie to relax.

"You mean, blanket, and that's a dated expression.
If you want to sound modern, try saying 'don't be such
a big fat pain.'"

They both ended up chuckling.

Such an unlikely pair they were. Hallie's well en-
dowed figure was four inches taller than her five-foot-
four friend who possessed a small framed body.

The French girl had a chic hairdo of short, dark
brown curls that shaped her Gallic head. Hallie's chin
length blond hair had been styled in a beveled cut to
look ruffled. It required little care which was the whole
point.

The differences didn't end there.

Where Hallie donned the cheapest blouse and skirt
she could find in the bargain barrels at Tati's, whenever
Monique was out of school and they went on longer
outings to Chartres or Mont St. Michel to visit the famous abbey, she always wore Italian designer clothes.

"*Salut* everyone!"

Paul, Monique's twin brother, joined them on the terrace and kissed them on both cheeks. At a lean six feet,

he was as good looking as his sister. Both twins wore their clothes well. Today he was dressed in a Polo shirt and jeans. Give him another eight to ten years and he would be a very attractive man.

He and Monique acted at home here. Maybe Hallie was being too cautious, but she knew the twins attended the very top private schools. With such strict rules, she didn't want to be the reason they bent them. It would be a shame to ruin their good records at the midnight hour.

"Thank goodness, you've arrived, Paul. Hallie thinks we shouldn't be here. She's ready to fly the croup!"

"Coop," came Hallie's automatic response. "That's another expression you need to throw out. If you want to be hip, I'd better buy you the latest book of idioms. Unfortunately by the time you've memorized it, all of them will be dated, too."

Paul laughed. "You're here now and we're not letting you go until we've had a toast to celebrate your birthday. Come with me."

They followed him into the dining room where he filled three wineglasses with golden liquid. The label on the bottle featured the Rolland name.

He lifted his glass. "To you, Hallie, for making this year unforgettable. May this be your happiest birthday!"

They all clicked glasses.

Hallie didn't drink alcohol, but she took a sip so she wouldn't offend them. They'd planned this little party in her honor. She was touched to realize they'd gone to so much trouble.

Before she left Paris she would write them a final letter of goodbye and wish them a happy life. So why not enjoy this unexpected moment of camaraderie while they were still together.

Monique excused herself for a moment, then returned with a gaily wrapped package Paul must have brought with him.

Hallie put her glass on the table so she could open it. Inside was a beautiful chiffon designer scarf in a café-au-lait and white print. "It will look nice with your brown skirt."

Emotion made her throat swell. "It's lovely, Monique." Hallie tied it around her neck in order to please her. "But you shouldn't have done it."

"I would have given you a lot more things, but I knew you wouldn't accept them. At least you can wear it for the rest of the time you work at Tati's."

"I'll always treasure the memory of this day," Hallie said, not wanting to argue the point. She would mail it back to Monique with the letter; she shouldn't be spending her money on presents.

The French girl cocked her head. "It looks very elegant with that white blouse you're wearing."

"It'll look elegant with my other blouses, too."

"I know. They're all white," Monique quipped.

Suddenly the three of them were laughing. They had a healthy sense of humor. Hallie loved them and was feeling the sense of loss more keenly than ever.

She wasn't supposed to form attachments, but they'd happened anyway. First in San Diego where she'd roomed with Gaby Peris before coming to France.

Gaby, a widowed immigration attorney who'd shared an apartment with Hallie to cut down on expenses, was now married to Max Calder, an ex-CIA agent. They had a new baby girl whom Hallie had only seen in pictures. *They'd named her Hallie.*

"Now, if you two will excuse me, I'll be back in fifteen minutes."

Hallie eyed Monique with a puzzled expression. "We just got here. Why are you leaving?"

"She's going to her favorite shop before it closes, aren't you," Paul insisted with a strange smile.

"That's right. À bientôt—see you in a bit."

After Monique disappeared, Hallie turned to Paul. "You're both acting very mysteriously."

He rubbed his palms together. "If we are it's because I wanted to be alone with you."

"Why?"

"So I can do something I've been wanting to do for a long time."

"What's that?"

"This."

In the next breath he cupped her face in his hands and kissed her lightly on her closed lips.

It came as such a complete surprise for all the obvious reasons, she decided to treat it as one of Paul's little jokes. He was a terrible tease on occasion.

"Wow! My last kiss before I go into seclusion. You've definitely made this birthday unforgettable."

"I've been wanting to do that for a long time," he confessed. "Now close your eyes. I have something else to give you."

"I think you've done enough for one day," she cautioned, but he ignored her. In a lightning gesture he reached for her left hand and slid something cool and metallic on her ring finger.

Her smile faded when she glimpsed the square-cut aquamarine stone mounted in yellow gold. The gem had to be three carats at least!

The sheer clarity and color made her gasp.

Even if it was an imitation, it must have cost a lot of money. More than was prudent even for someone of Paul's resources. When he knew what she was all about, it defied logic he actually meant her to have it.

What was he thinking?

She started to ask him, but the look of desire in his eyes stopped her cold.

"Happy twenty-fifth birthday, *ma belle*."

Hallie blinked. Paul was serious.

She sensed he was trembling. Gone was the fun loving, lighthearted banter she'd always associated with him.

How long had this been going on?

In her attempt to be there for the twins as part of her service in the outreach program, she hadn't realized he'd become infatuated with her. If there'd been telltale signs, she hadn't read them.

"It's a gorgeous piece of jewelry, but you'll have to return it."

"Don't be silly." He grasped her hands tighter so she couldn't remove it. "Even if you don't wear it, I want you to keep it as a constant reminder of me."

"I can't do that, Paul. You *know* why. Material things don't matter to me. When I enter the convent, I won't be taking anything with me."

His eyes had grown suspiciously bright. "I'm counting on your *not* entering. I adore you, Hallie—" he cried with all the ardency of a lovestruck teen.

"I'm staying in Paris as long as it takes to talk you into coming home to St. Genes with me. You weren't meant to be a nun. One day I hope you'll become my wife."

His wife—

He pulled her close with surprising strength. This

time he gave her a man's kiss filled with the heat of passion.

She couldn't believe it!

"Paul—" She pushed her hands against his chest to separate them, but he was so strong! Right now she prayed for inspiration to know how to reject him without hurting his pride.

"What in the name of heaven is going on here?"

A deep masculine voice permeated the stillness. Paul sprang away from her, flushing guiltily.

Hallie, on the other hand, was still so dazed at the depth of Paul's feelings for her—feelings he'd kept hidden until today—she was much slower to react to the interruption. All this time she'd thought of him like she might a younger brother.

"Papa—I thought you were in London," he said in a subdued tone.

"Obviously," came the terse reply. "*I* had the ridiculous impression my children might enjoy a celebration dinner with me this evening. But it appears your taste runs to something much stronger indeed."

There could be no doubt from his acid tone that Vincent Rolland had come into the dining room, that he'd caught his eighteen year old kissing a strange woman, that he'd seen the wine bottle and glasses on the table.

The evidence was so incriminating, Hallie shook her head. It just couldn't be worse for Paul, yet she really wasn't surprised. She shouldn't have ignored her earlier intuition that the twins had no business skipping school or bringing her to their father's apartment.

Hallie simply hadn't expected the man himself to arrive from England at the precise moment his son chose to reveal his affection for her.

Curiosity caused her to look across the expanse at Monsieur Rolland. She found herself staring at him.

The twins had shown her pictures of their father, but the camera hadn't captured his disturbing sensuality. She hadn't thought it possible any man could be more attractive than the new husband Hallie had lost in that horrendous plane crash two years ago. But she was wrong...

The twins had inherited their father's dark hair and brown eyes. However there was none of their innocence in his piercing eyes as his gaze swept over her, assessing her feminine attributes for a long serious moment.

Hallie had been the object of men's attention since her teens and had learned to live with it. However this man seemed to be looking for something beyond the physical. In the unremarkable blouse and brown skirt she was wearing, the designer scarf must appear ludicrously out of place.

He advanced into the dining room, his bronzed hands on his hips. Dressed in a pale blue knit shirt and cream colored jeans that molded his powerful thighs, his masculinity threw her senses into upheaval.

Closer now she could see his rock-hard physique topped Paul by several inches.

He picked up the wine bottle. One black brow slanted in displeasure. ''I can't fault your choice of vintage, but on a Thursday evening when you're supposed to be celebrating the end of school with your classmates?'' He finally put the bottle back on the table.

Paul cleared his throat. ''Hallie's birthday is much more important than being with a bunch of guys. Papa—may I introduce my friend, Mademoiselle Linn. We met last fall.''

Lines darkened his arresting features as he examined

her face and hair once more. Then his gaze dropped lower until it came to rest on the aquamarine stone shimmering on her finger.

"Ms. Linn," he muttered icily, insultingly, as if even having to acknowledge her presence was something he could scarcely tolerate.

Hallie was confused. Surely seeing her being kissed by his son didn't warrant such venom. In fact, she had the idea this display of hostility was a rare occurrence.

Determined to smooth things over she said, "How do you do, Monsieur Rolland. Your children have sung your praises for so long, I'm glad to have this opportunity to meet you at last."

"Papa? Could we go in the salon for a moment?"

"No, we could not." The quiet rage boiling beneath the surface was unmistakable. His eyes, more black than brown, remained fastened on the ring. "Since Mademoiselle Linn is such an intimate part of your life, I see no reason to exclude her from this conversation."

"It's true that I'm in love with her," he explained. "She means everything to me. In time I intend to marry her."

Paul!

Not only was she years older in age and experience, he had to be in complete denial.

A pulse throbbed along his father's jawline. "How very interesting… Now I understand why she's wearing a piece of jewelry that caused you to withdraw the entire balance of your checking account for the school year!"

Hallie moaned.

Paul displayed the classic symptoms of a rich young man whose infatuation had led him to make a very foolish and costly mistake.

"I'll always remember that you wanted to give me

this ring, Paul, but you know the reasons why I couldn't possibly accept it.''

She'd wanted to protect his sensitivities, but he'd gone too far and needed a wakeup call. Without hesitation she pulled the ring off her finger and put it on the table.

His face went ashen.

''It's too late to try to impress me with a 'you never meant to keep it', Ms. Linn.''

Paul wheeled around. ''You don't understand. I can explain!''

''I'll bet you can,'' his father bit out. ''Just as you can explain how many times you've brought her to my apartment since last fall.''

''I've never been here before this evening,'' Hallie addressed him in a quiet voice.

Right now she wasn't concerned for herself. It was his debilitating anger toward Paul that worried her. Monsieur Rolland had every reason to be upset, but the man was livid. To humiliate his son in front of her was doing much more harm than good.

''Of course you haven't.'' He sent her a mocking smile. ''Just as you had no idea that stone is the real thing.'' His eyes impaled her. ''I wonder what else you've managed to wangle out of him.''

Such cynicism explained Monique's remarks earlier. Like father, like daughter.

Hallie eyed him without flinching. ''I'd be happy to discuss this with you, but I think you should talk to your son alone first.''

His glacial smile didn't reach his eyes. ''I'm not interested in what you think, Ms. Linn. The more you say, the more I'm convinced the ring is only part of an elaborate scheme of extortion only a brazen young woman of your obvious charms would dream up to keep him in your thrall.''

''Now wait just a minute,'' Paul cried. ''You have no right to speak to Halli—''

''Enough!'' His father silenced him. ''Do you think me a complete imbecile? Don't you ever shout at me like that again, and don't ever speak to me of rights. You've forfeited any of yours by abusing my trust.''

As if on cue Monique made her entrance. *''Me voici!''* she called from the foyer. ''I've returned. Your time is up, Paul. I'm giving you fair warning in case I'm interrupting anything…''

Monique's words set the seal on this incredible tableau of misunderstanding. The little monkey had aided and abetted her brother so he could be alone with Hallie. It was a total revelation to her.

She couldn't understand how the twins would think she could have a romantic interest in Paul, who was so much younger. To spend all these months with her and still not appreciate her commitment to the vocation she'd chosen to follow…

The more she thought about it, the more she supposed it was a case of two idealistic young people believing what they wanted to believe.

From what they'd told Hallie, their mother had died in childbirth. After being separated from their father this last year, no matter how hard he'd tried to be an attentive parent and stay in close contact with them, they'd clung to Hallie. And *this* was the result!

''So—the prodigal daughter returns to the scene of the crime loaded with more clothes than are humanly decent.''

The moment Monique entered the dining room, her face turned to a study in bewilderment. She came to a standstill in front of her father. "Papa," she murmured, clearly shocked by his presence. "I thought you wouldn't be here until tomorrow."

"Obviously." He clipped out. "Otherwise this clandestine little arrangement would have gone undetected. What is it, nine months now that Ms. Linn has been given carte blanche to exploit my children and their propensity for handing over their material goods, which you've conveniently forgotten I provide?" he thundered.

"I'm surprised you had enough money left to purchase anything at all!" He plucked the box from under Monique's arm and opened it. Out slithered a flaming red cocktail dress. "Is this another contribution to the impoverished Ms. Linn?"

Hallie didn't think her blouse and skirt looked that bad.

"She's obviously doing very nicely by you two. Let's see…a designer scarf, a Givenchy dress and a nine thousand dollar ring."

Nine thousand dollars—

Her shocked gaze met his.

"That's quite a haul for one day's work, Ms. Linn." The skin around his lips had turned a noticeable white.

"Papa—" Monique gasped, shaking her head. Tears filled her eyes. "What's wrong? You are totally mistaken about everything, *mon pere.*"

He straightened to his full height. "It seems my daughter as well as my son has been thoroughly duped. You *do* know the meaning of the word, as in taken—conned—" His chest heaved.

"By Hallie?" Monique cried. "Impossible!" She stamped her foot, a habit of hers when she took a stand. "This was a surprise birthday party for her. She knew nothing! In fact she was so worried we might get into trouble, she almost didn't come in the taxi with me.''

"But she did come," her father rejoindered. "Take a good look. Until a moment ago she was wearing a small fortune and thanking your brother in that age old feminine way that leads a man to his destruction.''

His reaction didn't add up to the man the twins idolized. That person was a success in his business affairs, and a hero to his family. The unbending male standing a few feet from her bore little resemblance to the paragon of her imagination.

"Don't you realize she's made utter fools of you both, and gives me great cause to reflect on my own effectiveness as a parent," he ground out.

Hallie heard agony in his voice just now. In spite of his anger, it tugged at her.

"You two will go downstairs now, and take a taxi back to your schools. I'll visit you after I've had a little chat with Ms. Linn.''

The combination of pain and bitterness in Paul's eyes caused Hallie to fear for the relationship between him and his father.

Paul's anger was more frightening than his parent's because he was young and vulnerable, and had been caught redhanded at a very precarious moment in his life. It would take him much longer to forgive his father.

Her heart sank when he stormed out of the dining room and Monsieur Rolland let him go.

Monique stared up at her father like she'd never seen him before. Then her injured glance shifted to Hallie. "I'm sorry," she mouthed the words before hurrying after her brother.

The minute Hallie heard the elevator doors close she said, ''Please don't let them leave this way. Run after them quickly and apologize before any more damage is done!''

CHAPTER TWO

VINCENT ROLLAND'S eyes glittered with menace.

"It's a little late to be talking about damage, particularly if you're *pregnant*. But Paul couldn't know of your secret yet, otherwise he would never have left here without you."

Whoa. "Haven't your children ever mentioned me to you? Not even once?"

He looked like a man who'd had about all he could take.

"I didn't know of your existence until I saw my son kissing you with enough passion to convince me he's moved way beyond rational thought.

"I'm warning you now, Ms. Linn— No woman is going to trap my son into a travesty of a marriage and put him in bondage for the rest of his mortal life.

"If you're pregnant, you'll never have the opportunity to blackmail him. Before morning you'll be on a plane to wherever you came from with enough money to satisfy even your colossal greed."

This was a side of the twins' father she doubted they knew anything about. Perhaps he was wealthier than Hallie had imagined. Naturally he would want to be certain his children weren't being preyed upon. But to assume she was pregnant and accuse her of manipulating his son without giving her or Paul a chance to explain, fueled her anger.

"I'm not pregnant. But if I were, are you telling me you would bribe me into going away, *knowing* I was carrying your grandchild inside my body?'' she asked incredulously. ''You would deprive Paul of his own child to love and raise?''

A harsh laugh came out of him. ''Who said anything about it being Paul's?''

All these months Hallie had secretly revered the twins' father, but no longer.

''Be careful before you say anything else you'll live to regret, *monsieur*. Paul took us both by surprise today, but since *you* weren't capable of listening to reason, I fear your reaction will have caused real damage to your relationship with him.

''The truth is, I had no idea he'd developed a crush on me. Boys do that on occasion around an older woman. However I didn't realize it until a few minutes before you walked in.''

''It's hardly a crush, Ms. Linn,'' he retorted bleakly, appearing older all of a sudden. ''The reality of the ring and everything it entails puts this whole matter in a different light.

''Too many afternoon cocktail parties have a way of turning a boy's head and dissipating his brain. Particularly when a predatory female who looks like you supplies that extra *je ne sais quoi*.''

''*Je ne sais quoi?*'' Hallie mimicked the words as she untied the scarf and laid it on the table with the ring. ''That 'little extra something' is a dated expression Americans acquired years ago. Your daughter uses them constantly.''

He moved closer, putting his hands on his hips once more. A grimace darkened his features. Even in his anger, he was so attractive she was alarmed to find herself distracted by his potent sensuality.

''Who are you? What are you doing in Paris? How

did my children meet you?'' he fired one question after another.

"I'm someone who has been a friend to the twins."

"You expect me to believe that?" he lashed out.

"Yes. Just as I believe anything you tell me would be the absolute truth, too. Monique is like you in so many ways. But you'd be wise to watch your words because your cynicism has rubbed off on her.

"She was sure her headmistress wouldn't get her into trouble with you because, to quote your daughter, 'the woman is still trying to seduce you.' Sorry to be blunt, but dated expressions don't have quite that *je ne sais quoi* with me anymore.

"And one more thing. I don't care if you're as rich as King Midas! Since your son hasn't worked in the vineyards for the last school year, then leaving nine thousand dollars in his account is entirely too much money for an impulsive eighteen year old to handle, no matter how trustworthy he's been up until now."

"Are you quite finished?"

"Not yet," she said, ignoring his withering tone. "Let's just be thankful he tested the waters with me because I love your son like I would a younger brother. I care about his welfare.

"Paul doesn't realize it yet, but I'm part of a fantasy in his mind. He's confused right now. Give him a few more years and he'll have figured everything out.

"Do you know he wants to be exactly like you when he's grown up?" she drove the point home. "Self-assured, desirable to women, a success in life? For your information he did everything right when he toasted me with wine from your vineyards and wished me a happy birthday.

"No one could have been more charming or gallant.

And even though he trembled when he kissed me, he didn't hesitate. In fact he was very masterful when he reached for my hand and slid that ring on my finger.

"In ten years or so years he's going to make some lucky woman a wonderful husband in every way that counts. He shows all the promise, but he's still young and capable of being wounded because you shamed him in front of me.

"Surely you must know how much you hurt him by not letting him talk to you in private. I don't understand you, not when I think you've raised the most wonderful children I've ever met. That's why I stopped short of slapping your face."

Silence followed her last remark. He studied her for a long moment. "Before I have you investigated, why don't you answer my questions."

Investigated— He would go that far?

"Paul already told you. My name is Hallie Linn. Today I turned twenty-five, not eighteen! Until your children decided to surprise me with a little birthday celebration, I'd forgotten about it.

"We met last fall when they came into Tati's where I work. They were looking for birthday gifts for you, but were sticking to their budget. I asked them to describe you to me before I suggested a pair of gloves and a wallet."

She could tell by a flicker in the recesses of his dark eyes that he remembered receiving those gifts.

"They were surprised to find an American working there and loved trying out their English on me. In fact they begged me to correct their mistakes. I was charmed by their earnestness and their adoration of you. It was Papa this, and Papa that.

"Before they left the store, they asked if they could

come back the next week and practice their English with me again. I said yes, but didn't really expect to see them.

"Two days later they showed up and pled with me to spend my lunch hour with them. They'd brought sandwiches and drinks. I could hardly refuse, so we walked over to Notre Dame cathedral and had a little picnic.

"They spoke English the best they could and told me about life in St. Genes with you and their great grandfather Maurice. Oh yes, and Beauregard.

"At some point that afternoon the three of us became friends. It just happened. We've been close ever since. I should have recognized the signs of Paul's infatuation before today, but I didn't.

"I assume that's why they've never told you about me. It was wrong of them of course. But just now you treated their omission like they'd committed a sin. Why did you do that?"

He moved closer. "How did you get a job at Tati's?" His question proved he was too upset to be reasonable. "The government rarely issues work permits to Americans."

"They made an exception in my case, but don't be concerned. I'll only be depriving your countrymen of a job for another two weeks, then I'll be gone for good.

"As for your other fear, you've already solved that problem by coming to Paris to take your children home. Tell me something—if you're so distrustful of them, why did you send them away to boarding school?"

His lips twisted unpleasantly, but she was determined to make this last point.

"The twins could have gone to a perfectly good college in St. Genes so they could live at home with you where they belong. Life is so fleeting! Don't you know the love of a parent is more vital and necessary to a child than any expensive education?

"Your children worship you. They've missed you horribly and have studied hard to get the best grades so you'd be proud of them. I ought to know because I've spent hours tutoring them for their exams while we've explored Paris together on my days off.

"No doubt Monique bought that beautiful red dress to wear in front of you for Pere Maurice's birthday celebration next month. She claims every woman fantasizes about you.

"Though she hasn't said as much to me, I know she's worried that someone will come along you *do* want in your bed. Every day that she grows older, she's frightened she'll be replaced in your affection.

"Please—if there *is* a special woman in your life you haven't told them about either, don't let her be at the chateau when you take your children back to St. Genes. Give them your total attention first so they'll know nothing has changed.

"And please—promise me you'll work things out with Paul tonight before it's too late. He's trying hard to be a man. Go to him and explain why you were so upset. Paul's so sweet and sensitive inside. He'll understand and forgive you.

"*Adieu, monsieur. Que dieu vous benisse.*"

A few seconds later the elevator doors closed, leaving Hallie's words reverberating in the dining room.

Vincent remained frozen in place.

Like a master swordsman, she'd cut and thrust to produce a firestorm of emotions at the deepest level of his psyche. Then she'd had the audacity to bid him goodbye forever, imploring God to bless him.

He'd never met anyone remotely like her.

Never mind the womanly attributes that had blind-sided his son. What spell had this enigmatic stranger cast over both twins to evoke such singular affection?

For nine months their relationship had been flourishing without his knowledge. Vincent felt wounded. Betrayed.

He didn't buy the explanation that the twins had kept Ms. Linn's existence a secret in order to surprise him with their English proficiency.

No doubt Paul had fallen hard for her from the outset and had sworn Monique to secrecy. For a long time now she'd managed to infiltrate their world. No telling how many intimate details about his personal life and those of his children she'd elicited.

Though he didn't have the faintest clue who this American really was, he was going to find out.

He went to the study to look up the number of Tati's Department Store, then made a call to the manager. After being put on hold for a long time, someone in the credit department picked up and told him the manager had left for the day.

Vincent tried to get information about Ms. Linn, but was told he'd have to speak to the manager in the morning.

No sooner had he hung up, so he could call his attorney who would get the desired information for him, than his cell phone rang. The number of the chateau was displayed.

He clicked it on. "Vincent here."

"My boy...are you sitting down?"

Pere Maurice's sober question caused him to break out in a cold sweat. "What's wrong?"

"We just had a call from Passy Hospital in Paris. According to the police, Paul ran in front of a truck while he was crossing the boulevard against the light. They checked the ID in his wallet, then called here. He's still unconscious."

"I'm on my way!"

The short trip to the nearby hospital passed in a blur. He entered the emergency room on a run. The fear that Paul might not wake up had taken hold. Now it was Vincent imploring God to bless his son and keep him alive.

"Where have you put Paul Rolland?" he asked the staff worker at the admitting desk. "The police tell me he was hit by a truck. I'm his father."

"Your son is in cubicle five. You can go through those doors."

He pushed them open and hurried inside. The drawn curtain at number five caused his heart to drop like a stone. A nurse was just coming out.

"Is my son still unconscious?" he demanded without preamble.

"No. He woke up a few minutes ago."

Vincent could breathe again. "*Dieu merci*—oh, thank God."

"He's still being examined, but you can go in." The nurse pulled the curtain aside for him.

At first glance, Paul looked wonderfully alive despite his pallor. There was a goose egg at the side of his forehead near his hairline.

The doctor was cleaning an abrasion on his left cheek. He looked up as Vincent introduced himself

"Your son is a lucky young man. There are contusions on his left arm and leg, but no broken bones. The X-ray shows he has suffered a concussion, but with a few days bed rest the dizziness will pass and he'll be fine. I'll arrange to have him moved to a private room."

Those words brought exquisite relief. "Thank you for everything," he said before the doctor left the cubicle.

Now that they were alone, Vincent snagged a stool with his shoe and rolled it over to the examining table. He sat down next to Paul whose eyes had been closed the whole time.

"My son." He reached for his right hand. "It's Papa. I'm here. Thank God you're going to be all right!" his voice shook.

Paul didn't respond.

"Paul? Say something to me." His throat swelled. "I love you."

"No you don't."

The hurtful retort issued between taut lips sounded so cold, Vincent was crushed.

"Leave me alone. I don't want you here." He found the strength to pull his hand from his father's grasp.

Vincent's spirits plummeted to new depths. "That's your anger talking. You know I would never leave you. You're my son. I plan to stay with you until you're out of the hospital and I can take you and Monique home with me."

Paul's eyes opened once more, but there was no sign of warmth in those dark remote depths, or in his facial expression. The son Vincent had loved and raised from birth was nowhere to be found.

"I'm not going to St. Genes. That's over. I plan to stay in Paris. Don't worry. I've already arranged for a job and a place to live. You won't have to provide for me ever again,'' he tossed Vincent's words back at him with a bitterness that went marrow deep.

A grimace broke out on Vincent's face. ''I know I said a lot of things in the heat of the moment, Paul, and I apologize for them. When you're feeling better, we'll have that talk you wanted.''

''It's too late. We're finished. I never want to see you again.'' His eyelids fluttered closed, dismissing his father.

Letting out a sigh of remorse for having brought on this impasse Vincent said, ''We'll talk about things later. Right now the only thing that matters is that you recover.''

If Paul heard him, he made no further comment.

Deciding it was better to let him rest, Vincent used the cubicle phone to put through a credit card call to Pere Maurice and let him know Paul was going to be all right. The old man wept with relief. Fortunately he hadn't tried to reach Monique who knew nothing about the accident yet.

They talked for a few more minutes, then Vincent followed the orderlies who took Paul to a private room on the third floor. While a nurse took his vital signs, another doctor came in the room and shook hands with Vincent.

''I'm Dr. Maurois. If you'd step outside in the hall for a moment, I'd like to talk to you about your son's case.''

Vincent complied, but his senses were on alert that something was wrong. He eyed the man grimly. ''Are there complications I haven't been told about?''

''I'm afraid so. However the attending physician felt it best that you hear the details from me. I'm the head of the psychiatric department here at Passy Hospital.''

The doctor might as well have driven a fist into Vincent's gut. "Go ahead. I'm listening."

In the next few minutes he heard news no parent ever wants to hear.

"If you'd prefer another psychiatrist, feel free to find someone else."

"I'm sure you're well qualified," Vincent murmured. "Heaven knows my son needs help. The sooner, the better."

The psychiatrist nodded. "What are your plans for the next few days?"

"To stay here with my son. My daughter Monique, his twin, will be joining me."

"Good. For the time being, don't mention what I've told you to him or your daughter. Only say and do the things that come naturally. I'll be talking to him at regular intervals over the next forty-eight hours, then I'll meet with you and your daughter, both together and individually. We'll go from there."

"Thank you," Vincent said in a dull voice.

Once the nurse assured him Paul was resting comfortably, Vincent left to drive over to Monique's school.

Before going to her room, he went to the office and thanked the headmistress for watching out for his daughter. She told him it had been a pleasure. She also invited him to come by any time when he happened to be in Paris on business. Her eyes held a private invitation he couldn't possibly misconstrue.

After hearing Ms. Linn repeat Monique's words revealed in confidence about the headmistress, he found himself repulsed by her blatant offer.

There'd been several women over the years he'd enjoyed when he'd gone out of town on business. But the headmistress would never be one of them.

Still in shock after learning what Dr. Maurois had to say, his heart sank further to discover Monique in her bedroom lying prostrate on the bed. Her tear-ravaged cheeks devastated him. He'd seen her like this before, but never because of something *he'd* done. It cut him to the core.

Riddled by guilt on so many counts, he sat down on the bed and put his arms around her. "I'm sorry, *mon cherie*. So sorry." He rocked her for a while. "One day I hope you and Paul will be able to forgive me."

Like Paul, she remained mute. What had he done?

Aware that Paul had been left alone he eventually said, "Come on. We need to get back to the hospital. Let's carry your things out to the car. There's something important I have to tell you, but I don't want to talk about it until we're away from the school."

On that note his puffy-eyed daughter helped him load the trunk with her cases which she'd already packed in anticipation of leaving school for good. En route to the hospital he turned to her. "How come you and Paul didn't share a taxi back to your schools?"

"He took off running. I couldn't stop him. But I have to tell you—I don't blame him for what he did, Papa."

Monique was fiercely loyal to Paul. Vincent loved his daughter for it.

"Neither do I. Unfortunately your brother was so upset, he met with an accident." It was the truth, just not all of it. That wouldn't come until Dr. Maurois felt the time was right. "But he's going to be fine," he added the second he heard her frightened cry.

"No broken bones. Only concussion. In a few days he'll be able to travel. The problem right now is, he thinks he hates me, and he has every right.

"Before we spend the night with him, I want to hear

all about Hallie Linn. Don't leave anything out. And don't worry, I'm not asking because I suspect her of something sinister.

"However I do need to know about your relationship with her so I can understand what's going on inside of Paul. I love your brother. But until I hear all the facts, I won't be able to truly apologize to him in a way that he'll accept as genuine. Do you know what I'm saying?"

"I don't think this is something you can fix, *mon pere*."

Coming on the heels of Dr. Maurois's gut wrenching news, her opinion alarmed him. She sounded too grave and final about it.

Some time during the last nine months, his children had grown up. He hadn't been there to see it happen and felt searing pain. Not only for what he'd missed, but for what he'd caused to happen.

"I have to try."

"Paul's been in love with her since the first day she waited on us at Tati's. I could see why. She's perfect! I totally approve of her for my future sister-in-law."

"What makes her so special?"

"She's the only person I feel is worthy of Paul's love."

Worthy?

Coming from Monique who was a twin and crazy about her brother almost to the point of being possessive of him, those were powerful words. He needed to tread carefully.

Since Vincent had married at eighteen, right now wasn't the time to raise the issue that Paul was too young to know the difference between infatuation and love.

Without sounding like a hypocrite, how could he tell his daughter that Paul would probably be in love four or five times until he'd reached his mid to late twenties?

A man needed to be that age before he became a responsible adult with a viable career. Only then could he hope to find the kind of stability needed to achieve a happy marriage with the right woman.

"Paul would have told you about her a lot sooner, but he was afraid you wouldn't approve of his falling in love with an American. He asked me not to say anything about her until he was ready."

Vincent knew in his gut that wasn't the reason his son had kept him in the dark. He shifted gears to pass a car. "I have no bias against Americans. I admit there was one client who came here a few years ago I didn't particularly care for, but on the whole I find most of my American acquaintances quite charming."

He sucked in his breath. "My reaction to Ms. Linn had nothing to do with her nationality. I was in shock to think Paul had spent the money on a ring rather than a car designated for your graduation gift."

His daughter lowered her head. "He was determined to get engaged by the end of the school year. I told him I didn't care about a car. If he wanted to spend that money on her, it was fine with me.

"In case you're worried, he plans to pay you back in monthly installments. His headmaster gave him a reference and he used that to get an entry level job at a bank in Montparnasse. He's supposed to start his training on Monday."

Incredible.

Tomorrow Vincent would go over to Paul's school for his things. While there he would phone the bank and let the manager know about Paul's accident.

"I had a talk with Ms. Linn after you two left the apartment, petite. Though she looks younger to me, she says she's twenty-five."

"She is. Paul saw the inside of her passport."

"Don't you think a woman seven years older than your brother is too old for him?"

"Of course not," she answered back, but it was a little too fast even for Monique. "Paul finds her totally fascinating."

And because you love your twin, you're not about to sabotage his plans.

Vincent rubbed the back of his neck in consternation. He wagered there weren't too many females in all of Paris with Ms. Linn's fascinating feminine attributes. With those long legs, she had a voluptuous physical allure that didn't require expensive clothes to draw a man's attention.

As far as he could tell, she wore no makeup. After she'd removed the scarf, he'd noticed a small cross hanging around her neck, but he'd seen no other jewelry.

Except for the ring she'd removed in his presence.

"Paul thinks my girlfriends at school are shallow and boring. I happen to agree with him. Hallie has had experiences that make her different from other people. She's the best listener in the world."

With a woman who looked like Ms. Linn hanging on Paul's every word, he never stood a chance.

"Does she have family here in Paris?"

"No. She was born in California, but she's all alone in the world now."

"I see." He pursed his lips. "Tell me about these experiences that have made her so unique in your eyes."

"I don't know the details because it's hard for her to talk about them, but she was in a plane crash a few years ago. It made her reassess her values. She decided she wanted to help people."

"That's an admirable desire," he murmured, trying to keep the condescension out of his voice.

Out of all the people his children could have met in Paris, how did they happen to run into this particular woman?

"What brought her to Paris?"

"Her work."

"You mean there's a Tati's in California, and she was transferred here?"

Monique shook her head. "No."

Vincent gripped the steering wheel tighter. He'd played at this conversation long enough. "Why do I get the feeling you're afraid to answer my question?"

"Paul asked me not to tell you."

"If she's so perfect, then why the concern?"

"Because he knows the answer will make you happy."

His daughter was speaking in riddles. More puzzled than ever, Vincent pulled into the hospital parking and shut off the engine.

"Am I such an awful ogre you can no longer trust me with the truth?" He needed all the truth his daughter could give him in order to work with Dr. Maurois.

She slowly turned her head toward him. The tortured brown eyes so dear to him seemed to take up her whole face.

"In two weeks Hallie's going back to California to enter a convent."

A convent.

Ms. Linn?

"Paul can't bear it," her voice trembled. "That's why he gave her the ring, so she'd know he was serious about getting married one day. He'd do anything to stop her from making a decision that will prevent him from seeing her again. If you knew how wonderful Hallie was yo—"

"Just a minute," he cut her off. "Back up." Vincent's mind was reeling. "She told you she *intends* to become a nun?"

Talk about dangling forbidden fruit in front of Paul! Could anything the opportunistic Ms. Linn have dreamed up to bring him to his knees have worked better than a fabrication like that?

"Papa— Hallie already *is* a lay nun."

"Then she's been lying to you," he muttered through gritted teeth.

"No," Monique protested in a calm voice. "She's been doing church service for the last year and a half through the Dominicans. First in California, then at Clairemont Abbey not far from Tati's.

"Nowadays more and more women are working as lay nuns in ordinary clothes while they mingle with the public. They hold day jobs to pay for their own housing and expenses."

This was the first Vincent had heard of it. Whether it was true or not, Monique firmly believed Ms. Linn's story. Until he could check it out, he didn't dare alienate his daughter any further.

He took a fortifying breath. "All right. Assuming everything she's told you is true, why is she suddenly leaving Paris?"

His daughter looked crestfallen. "She has plans to take her vows at the motherhouse in San Diego in June. The only problem is, once she's professed we'll never see her again.'' The tremor in her voice revealed such deep affection, it stunned Vincent.

''Paul's desperate to keep her here. He loves her so much. It isn't like he has a few years to work on her and get her to change her mind before proposing. He had to do it now, today, before it was too late! It's taken him months to get up the courage.

''We planned the birthday fete in order to bring her to the apartment where he could have privacy when he asked her to marry him. Since he needed time alone, I left them long enough to buy Etvige a dress with the last of the money I'd been saving. She's always wanted something stylish from Paris.''

His daughter's explanation plunged him further into the black hole engulfing him since his conversation with Dr. Maurois. While she was talking, he could hear another voice from another conversation, drowning out her words.

''I'm not pregnant. But if I were, are you telling me you would bribe me into going away knowing I was carrying your grandchild inside my body? You would deprive Paul of his own child to love and raise?''

A harsh laugh came out of him. *''Who said anything about it being Paul's?''*

''Be careful before you say anything else you'll live to regret. Paul took us both by surprise today, but since you were incapable of listening to reason, I fear your reaction has caused irrevocable harm to your relationship with him.

''Promise me you'll work things out with him tonight before it's too late. He's trying hard to be a man. Go to him and explain why you were so upset. Paul's very sweet and sensitive inside. He'll understand and forgive you.''

Vincent groaned. His assessment of the situation had been so completely off the mark, he felt like he'd entered the twilight zone with no exit.

In reality there *was* no exit, not after what the psychiatrist had told him.

Paul's mental health was in grave jeopardy. Furthermore Vincent had permanently destroyed the bond with his son, a bond he'd once thought to be indestructible. What made things even more hopeless— he couldn't help Paul if he wanted to where Ms. Linn was concerned.

She wasn't in love with his son.

If Vincent recalled her words correctly, she'd said she loved Paul like a younger brother. Before leaving the dining room she'd murmured "Goodbye forever. May God bless you."

Something about those parting words convinced Vincent she'd been telling his children the truth. She'd meant what she'd said in the literal sense because she would be turning her back on the world when she took her vows.

Everything that had transpired at his apartment was starting to make a horrible kind of sense. The Rolland household had been turned inside out.

Monique was barely speaking to him. His son was in hell because Vincent had insulted the love of his life, a woman who was about to become cloistered and permanently unavailable to him.

Everything Vincent had done since the twins' birth to make sure they didn't repeat his mistakes had blown up in his face.

Nothing would ever be the same again.

Had it only been twelve hours since he'd awakened

in his hotel room in London, excited because he was going to fly to Paris to surprise his beloved children?

Tonight despair made him feel a thousand years old.

"Let's go inside, petite. Paul needs us, even if he wishes I were drawing my last breath in the middle of the Sahara." *Even if my son wishes he'd left this earth...*

CHAPTER THREE

IT WAS five o'clock on Saturday evening. Hallie took care of her last customer, rang up the receipts and left Tati's.

Two days had passed since she'd hurried out of Monsieur Rolland's apartment in pain. The terrible situation she'd unwittingly created by becoming friends with his children had been haunting her until she had to do something about the awful limbo she was in.

Last night she'd started a fast after her prayers. Tonight she had an appointment to talk with Mother Marie-Claire about the twins. By now they were home with their father in St. Genes. Hallie feared that any attempt on her part to talk to him or his children by phone would prove unsuccessful.

The only thing she could think to do was send him a letter conveying her sorrow, and hope he wouldn't tear it up without reading what was in her heart first. But before she put her thoughts to paper, Hallie wanted to know her Superior's opinion on the problem.

In the beginning Hallie had perceived she could fill a need for the twins while they were away from home. Tragically it had backfired with shattering consequences.

The painful encounter with their father had caused Hallie to lose confidence in her judgment as a human being, let alone as a nun. Where had the inspiration been to prevent this disaster?

Was she such a prideful person it had gotten in the

way because she'd believed it was her mission to comfort the motherless twins? Had it blinded her to signs of trouble?

Or was it some latent maternal instinct that had suddenly sprung to life, thus preventing her common sense from surfacing?

In either case, what kind of a nun was she going to make in the future working with young people?

This was one of the questions she needed answers to. If she didn't find some peace on the matter soon, Hallie feared she wouldn't be good for the order. Sick at heart, she started walking faster.

"Ms. Linn?"

Hallie knew that deep, masculine voice. She spun around in surprise that the twins' father was still here in Paris. Her heart skipped several beats.

She'd wanted another chance to talk to him and try to make things right. His presence meant that one of her wishes had been granted at least.

He'd pulled his car up to the curb not far from Tati's. It was like déjà vu if she remembered Monique waiting for her in the same spot two nights ago. Except that he got out of his vehicle to approach her.

This evening he was dressed in a lightweight gray suit. It provided the perfect foil for his dark, handsome looks. But as he drew closer, she felt he'd aged since their confrontation.

Lines bracketed his mouth. His olive complexion seemed paler. She glimpsed pain in those deep set brown eyes made more remarkable by lashes black as jet.

Though he didn't stare at her with the same contemptuous disdain as before, she had no sense that his feelings were any friendlier toward her. More, it was a case of enough time having passed for the first white heat of anger to dissipate.

"Paul's in the hospital," he began without preamble.

Those were the last words she expected to hear. "What's wrong with him?" she cried in dismay.

"My son's not dying if that's what you're worried about. At least not from anything physical," came the muttered aside.

"Then what is it?"

She heard his sharp intake of breath. "He ran in front of a truck after he left the apartment the other evening."

"Oh no—" A shudder rocked her body.

"As I told you, he's going to be fine. All he sustained was a concussion and some bruises."

Her eyes closed tightly. "Thank heaven he's alive. He was so upset it doesn't surprise me he didn't watch where he was going."

"That's where you're wrong," he fired back. "When the paramedics brought him to the hospital, he was unconscious. He woke up in the emergency room thinking he'd died and had awakened on the other side.

"When the doctor told him he hadn't been killed and was very much alive, Paul didn't want to believe it. That's when he admitted he'd run in front of the truck on purpose."

"*What?*" Hallie couldn't bear it. "Paul really wanted to die?"

His tortured gaze reflected her horror. She felt his hand close over her elbow. "We need to talk, but we can't do it here. I presume you're off work?"

"Yes," she answered, feeling light-headed. "I was on my way…home." She would reschedule her visit with Mother Marie-Claire later. This was more important.

''Under the circumstances I'd prefer taking you to my apartment first. While we eat, I'll fill you in on what Paul's doctor had to say before I left the hospital this evening.''

She nodded, still shaken by the alarming news.

At her capitulation, his taut jaw appeared to relax somewhat. With his hand still on her arm, he ushered her past the flux of pedestrians to his car. It was an automatic gesture she was sure, but she felt the warmth of that contact radiate through her body.

No doubt she was unduly aware of him because she hadn't been with another man since her husband's death. During that unreal moment when they'd known their plane was going down, he'd crushed her in his arms one last time. Since then she'd been oblivious to other men.

After helping Hallie inside, Monsieur Rolland slid behind the wheel. Once he started the ignition, they entered the mainstream of traffic. For a few minutes there was silence between them.

''This is my fault for being unaware of Paul's feelings.''

''Before you start blaming yourself,'' he began in a low voice, ''you need to know there were many factors that conspired to bring on this crisis. Dr. Maurois, the psychiatrist who has been working with my son, drove that point home to me.

''According to him, no one is to blame. Beating ourselves up over what we perceive is our failure with Paul, for whatever reason, is a waste of negative energy and won't help the situation.''

She wiped the moisture off her cheeks. ''Have you been able to put your guilt away?'' Her voice throbbed with emotion she couldn't hide.

At first she thought he hadn't heard her because he took so long to answer.

"No," he finally whispered with such pain-filled honesty, she was wounded all over again.

Like the phoenix rising from the ashes, she'd been given a second chance after the plane crash to do something productive with her life.

At least that had been her goal.

Yet somehow all she'd managed to do was bring turmoil to the Rolland family. Ignorance was no excuse where the twins were concerned.

"I was supposed to have been the wise one. The person who brought a little light into a bad day, the one who supplied comfort by just being there and listening if Monique or Paul needed a sounding board. I simply didn't see this coming."

"You weren't the only one taken by surprise," their father exclaimed with self-recrimination. She could feel it permeate her being.

"I don't remember my mother," he continued, sounding very far away. "Only my father who kept me on a tight leash while I was growing up. He feared that if I ever left the vineyard, even for a short trip, I'd never be satisfied with home.

"My grandparents tried to intervene for me, but to no avail. For years I cursed my father and swore that if I ever had children, I would make certain they were exposed to new places and experiences.

"When I told the twins I was sending them to Paris to school—something I would have given anything to happen to me at their age—they seemed to be less than enthusiastic about leaving home. I couldn't believe they weren't leaping at the chance to embrace life."

He shot her a glance. "What an irony to think they

didn't want to go. But I was certain I was doing the right thing to give them a nudge out of the nest, believing it would be for their ultimate good.''

Hallie's heart was breaking. ''You were so open with the twins and gave them so much love, they didn't feel the need to get away. But they would never have hurt your feelings by telling you they wanted to go back home.''

''So they told *you* instead,'' his voice grated. ''I'm sorry you've had to shoulder the responsibility for my mistake all this time.''

''Don't ever say that!'' she cried. ''It wasn't a mistake. They had a marvelous time in Paris. The two of them experienced things that couldn't possibly have been learned in any other way.

''You have the most wonderful children in the world. I love them. I've loved every minute we've spent together.

''Their need to have a friend outside of school vindicated my work. You see before I came to France, I was going to take my vows. But like you, the holy mother felt her fledgling needed more time to be in the world.

''She wanted me to be absolutely certain about my vocation before I became a professed nun. Arrangements were made for me to work in the outreach program here in Paris. I didn't want to come. Then I met your children right away. It seemed like destiny.

''I was so intent on being there for them, I didn't realize Paul looked at me as anything but a friend. I didn't know…'' Her voice trailed.

The car accelerated. ''Have you forgotten I'm the one who turned into a monster and drove him from the apartment?'' he countered. ''Now my own daughter's so terrified of me she flinches whenever I start to talk to her. But that's all history.''

They didn't speak again until they'd reached his apartment in Passy. He showed her into the dining room. All traces of the birthday party had vanished. After telling her to sit down, he asked her what she'd like to eat.

''Nothing for me. Thank you anyway.''

His black brows formed a bar. ''But you must want something after working all day, Sister.''

''I'm not a sister yet, Monsieur Rolland. Not in the way you mean. Please call me Hallie.''

He studied her features for a moment. ''How about a mineral water?''

She could tell he was determined to be a good host. ''I'm still fasting.''

He raked an unsteady hand through the vibrant dark hair he wore medium length. ''Do you mind if I drink coffee in front of you? I think I need some caffeine.''

His courtesy revealed the side of his nature that had won his children's love from the beginning.

''Of course I don't mind, *monsieur*.''

''Call me Vincent.''

''All right.''

Two days ago she couldn't have imagined having a civil conversation with him.

''Please go ahead and eat dinner if you want. At a time like this you need to keep up your strength. I imagine you and Monique have been with Paul around the clock and are desperately tired.''

The fatigue lines near his eyes and mouth testified to his loss of sleep. ''We've been trading off in shifts so he's never alone.''

His penetrating gaze held hers for a long moment. She couldn't tell what he was thinking, but the intensity of that look left her shaken.

"The bruises beneath your eyes indicate you haven't slept, either," he finally remarked before disappearing into the kitchen.

While he was gone, she took advantage of the time to freshen up in the bathroom down the hall from the entry. When she returned to the dining room, she discovered him seated at the head of the table.

She watched him put two overflowing teaspoons of sugar into his coffee. Just then he cast her a searching glance.

"You look amused."

"Now I know where the twins get their sweet tooth. They never go anywhere without some kind of marzipan."

One corner of his mouth lifted, giving her a glimpse of the person he'd been before he'd walked in on her and Paul. "I was crazy about it as a boy."

Vincent Rolland would have been a good-looking boy. Now he was a breathtaking man.

Alarmed by her errant thoughts, she sat down in the chair next to him, anxious to talk about his son.

"You came to my work for a specific reason. If it's more information you want, I'll tell you anything, do anything I can to help." A heavy sigh escaped her throat. "I love Paul. His mental state takes precedence over all other considerations."

He drank his coffee in several long draughts before lowering the cup. "Do you love him enough to tell him you're going to spend the summer at Chateau Rolland?"

His question was the last thing she expected to hear.

"According to Dr. Maurois, in the ideal world where my son lives in his mind, that's what he's been wishing for with all his heart since he met you.

"Paul has no doubts that if you came to the Dordogne and spent time with him on a day to day basis, you would realize your true destiny doesn't lie in a convent with the other sisters."

She lowered her head. Paul's escape from death hadn't changed him. He still saw what he wanted to see.

"What does Dr. Maurois think?"

"To quote him, 'it might be the best thing that could happen.' It would be a case of familiarity breeding contempt. In the natural course of events Paul would discover you're not the perfect woman he has put on a pedestal.

"On the contrary, he would find you're a flesh and blood human being with the usual amount of weaknesses. He would see that your needs and interests weren't compatible with his own. In time he would get over his infatuation and move on. It's called, growing up, something he needs to do."

A long silence ensued while she digested everything the psychiatrist had said.

After lifting her eyes to Vincent she asked, "What do *you* think about his theory?"

"It's a moot point. You chose your path a long time ago. Nevertheless the doctor feels it's important that Paul sees you one more time so he won't remain under the impression I've done you some kind of harm."

He pushed himself away from the table and stood up, but not before she saw the glint of anguish in his eyes.

The man suffered from some inner turmoil. After being in the company of other lay nuns still struggling over personal issues, she recognized the signs.

"Surely Paul knows better than that."

A bleak expression entered his eyes once more. "Let's not pretend my anger didn't do lasting damage."

Hallie was sure there'd been a reason for it. Something terrible had happened in his past. Most likely it had to do with his despotic father. She shivered.

"Before I drive you to the hospital, you should know Paul hasn't spoken to me since the accident. I've had to rely on the doctor and Monique for information. I'm afraid she's as convinced as Paul that I've purposely kept you away from them."

Armed with that knowledge, Hallie got to her feet. She felt shaky, but couldn't attribute all of her weakness to fasting.

"Then I'll prove your children wrong."

She hadn't been able to stop Paul from trying to end his life. No one could have known what was in his mind when he'd left the apartment on Thursday. By some miracle his life had been preserved. Now he was getting the best professional help possible.

But no one was helping his father.

Beneath that urbane sophistication lived a fragile man right now. It was up to her to take the sword out of Paul's hand. She was the only one who could do it. Otherwise the precious father and son relationship they'd shared might never exist again.

"Hallie!" Monique cried in shock when she emerged from Paul's room and found Hallie outside in the corridor with her father. Relief and delight broke out on her face. They kissed on both cheeks.

"I've been wanting to come, Monique, but I had to

wait until Paul's doctor gave me permission to visit. Your father was kind enough to pick me up from work and bring me here. He told me there wasn't a moment to lose.''

At first the vivacious French girl looked uncertain as her dark gaze flicked to her father for confirmation. Then she hugged him. ''Merci, Papa. It'll make Paul so happy.''

Monique's forgiving nature warmed Hallie's heart. Vincent's eyes thanked her as their gazes met over the top of his daughter's head. ''We'll be waiting in the lounge around the corner when you're through.''

Hallie nodded before entering Paul's hospital room. Though the TV was on, he appeared to be asleep.

The interior felt too warm. She could understand why he lay on top of the covers. Vincent must have brought over the fancy striped pajamas he was wearing.

His dinner tray sat on the rolling bed table, uneaten. She moved to his side to examine the bruised remains of the goose egg which had gone flat. Her heart said a little prayer of thanksgiving that he was alive and looked as well as he did considering his ordeal.

''Paul? It's Hallie. I came as soon as the doctor would let me in to see you.''

The black lashed eyelids he'd inherited from his father flew open. ''Hallie—I didn't think I'd see you again. I—I can't believe it.''

''Why ever not?'' She leaned over and kissed him on his right cheek. ''I think we'll give your left one a rest.''

She was rewarded with the distinctive Rolland smile.

''Don't try to sit up. The doctor says you're still suffering some dizziness.''

''It's not as bad as it was.''

"Liar," she teased. "You haven't eaten your dinner."

"I'm not hungry. The hospital food is disgusting."

"Worse than your school's? I didn't think that was possible. Admit the cook at St. Genes spoiled you rotten."

"I admit it," he said, eyeing her steadily.

"Mind if I eat your dinner? I came here straight from work. Besides, it's time to end my fast."

He blinked. "You've been fasting?"

"That's right. For you and your family."

She pulled the chair around, then sat down with the tray and started eating.

"I decided the Rollands need all the help they can get right now. Your accident must have been especially hard on Pere Maurice who, according to you, was counting the minutes until you and Monique arrived at St. Genes. Have you talked to him today?"

"He's called twice."

"I'm sure it made him happy to hear your voice. Your accident gave everyone a huge scare. Especially me."

Paul lifted his head in spite of his dizziness. "How did you find out? Monique?"

"No. Your father. He came to my work and drove me here."

His countenance darkened. "How could you even speak to him after the way he treated you?"

"I've accepted his heartfelt apology. His only thought is your happiness."

"You have to say that because you're a nun," came the bitter aside.

"I was taught from childhood to forgive, Paul, no other reason. Your father's in terrible pain. You, better than anyone, know it's true. As for my being a nun, I'm not professed yet. That's what I'm here to talk to you about.''

Hallie hadn't cleared this with Mother Marie-Claire. She hadn't even had a moment to discuss it with her. But there were times when all Hallie had to go on was gut instinct. This was one of them.

Paul wasn't the only person whose emotional well being hung in the balance.

''First let me finish my dinner, then we'll talk. I'm going to tell you something you don't know about me.''

Alerted by the unexpected comment, he turned on his good side and waited.

She needed nourishment and ate quickly. Once she'd drained the glass of apple juice, she got up and put the tray on a small table placed against the wall. Then she went back to Paul and sat down. His gaze never left her face.

''This will come as a surprise to you. I've been married before.''

The revelation gave him a start. A hurt look slowly crept over his face as she'd known it would. Already one veil had been removed from his eyes. That was good.

''How come you never told us?'' he asked in a quiet voice.

''Because it was too painful. My husband died in the plane crash you've heard me talk about.''

He stared at her like he'd never seen her before. ''Did you love him?''

''Terribly. I raged against God that He didn't take me, too.''

She could see his throat working. ''Pere Maurice said

Papa loved our mother like that," he whispered. "I'm sorry, Hallie."

"It's all right. Since the plane crash, my life hasn't been easy, but today I can honestly say I'm not hurting anymore. As you can imagine, his death changed me in countless ways. I found solace working as a lay nun.

"There's a lot of suffering in the world, Paul. To be able to alleviate someone's burden no matter how small has helped take my mind off myself and brought me pleasure."

He moved onto his back. Looking up at the ceiling he said, "Were Monique and I one of your projects?"

"Yes," she answered honestly. "You were both missing home. I wanted to be there if you needed a person to talk to."

He switched his gaze back to her. Some of the light had faded from his eyes.

Another veil had been ripped away. At this point she needed to proceed with caution.

"Perhaps now you can understand the risk of being a lay nun. Sometimes in reaching out to others, attachments are formed on the part of the person being helped, as well as the helper. When that happens, it makes saying goodbye much more difficult.

"Paul—" She leaned forward. "I learned to love you and Monique, and I know you both love me. It wasn't supposed to happen, but it did.

"When your sister came for me on Thursday, I should have said no. If I were the kind of nun I'm supposed to be, I would have been able to put my duty first. But I didn't do that.

"Instead, I got in the taxi and went to your father's apartment because I didn't want to deny myself the pleasure of your company."

By now he'd elevated himself on one elbow, his avid eyes intent on her features.

"Do you know why I was sent to France?"

"No."

"After I'd formed a strong attachment to a friend in California, the holy mother at the convent there warned me I hadn't been a lay nun long enough to know my own mind. She urged me to give it another year before I took my vows and made arrangements for me to come here.

"It's obvious she knew something about me I didn't know about myself because history repeated itself. I became attached to you and Monique.

"The whole point of being a nun is to serve others without playing favorites. That's impossible to do if you're married and have a family. Since I no longer had a husband, I believed I had the right stuff to be of service. But maybe I don't.

"Little did I know you were going to ask me to marry you, Paul. Because I'd already been doubting my ability to be a good nun, you really shook me up when you said the religious life wasn't meant for me. It was like someone had walked over my grave."

Everything she'd told him was the truth. But saying it out loud threw her into more turmoil.

"I didn't mean it like that!" he cried.

"I know you didn't," she replied calmly. "But your words resonated with the part of me that realizes I'm still not ready to take my vows. Otherwise I wouldn't place so much value on my friendship with you and Monique.

"Therefore, I've made the decision to stay in France for a while longer. Hopefully in time I'll know my own mind and heart better."

"Hallie—"

The excitement in his voice alarmed her. At this point she prayed Dr. Maurois's theory would prove prophetic. Otherwise her decision could bring on worse consequences.

Yet Vincent wouldn't have told her about it if he hadn't thought the theory was sound. His desperation had touched her soul. If she could help mend the breach between him and Paul, it would do wonders to restore her morale.

"Since I won't have a job at Tati's after next week, I won't be able to stay in Paris. Fortunately the order has an outreach program in Lyon."

He frowned. "Lyon? Why would you go there?"

"A job, for one thing."

"You don't need to work. I'll take care of you. I'm starting a job at the Credit Montparnasse as soon as I get out of the hospital."

"That's what your father told me. But you don't understand. I'm still a lay nun here in France on a work visa. I have to show proof of employment in order to stay."

"Then come to St. Genes!" He moved his long muscular legs around so they hung over the side of the bed. "I'll get you a job in the winery office. Yves Brouard is the manager. He'd do anything for me."

"What about your new job?"

"I only got it to be near you. Since they haven't started to train me yet, I'll tell them I've changed my mind. You'll love the chateau. You can stay in any guest bedroom you want."

"No, Paul. If I were to come to St. Genes, I'd find a room in town to rent just like I do here in Paris."

His eyes held a speculative gleam. "The chateau has

a few outbuildings that used to be the servants' quarters in the 1800s. If Monique and I got one of the cottages ready for you, you could rent it through my father's estate manager, Bernard Artois. He and his family live in one.''

Paul thought of everything. Where there was a will…

''How far is the chateau from the main town?''

''Three kilometers.''

''I suppose if I bought a second hand bike to do errands, I could also get myself back and forth without any problems.''

His eyes lit up. ''Monique has several you could borrow.''

''Let's both sleep on it, shall we?'' She got to her feet.

''Don't go yet—''

''I have to. Doctor's orders. But I'll be back tomorrow. I hope you feel tons better in the morning. Good night.''

She slipped out of the room before he could think of another reason to detain her. Vincent and Monique stood up the minute they saw her in the lounge entry. They made a striking father and daughter combination.

''Would you mind running me home straight away? My apartment's near Tati's.''

''I was planning on it.'' His anxious eyes played over her features for some visible sign of the outcome of her visit with Paul.

''I'll drive with you, Papa.''

Before he could forestall his daughter Hallie said, ''When I left Paul, he was wide-awake and wants company. I don't know anyone who can cheer him up better than you. Here.'' She opened her purse and handed

Monique a marzipan bar. "I ate the dinner he didn't want, but I think he might go for this."

Monique laughed. "If he doesn't want it, I do."

Vincent's lips twitched. Every time Hallie saw a reaction like that, she wanted to see it happen again.

They went back down the hall to Paul's room. Vincent gave his daughter a hug. "I won't be long."

Turning to Hallie, he gripped her elbow and walked her to the elevator. She sensed his urgency to get her alone. However there were too many people packed inside who would be able to hear every word. She remained silent till they reached the car.

"You were in too long with Paul," he said as they headed out of the parking lot. "It must have been an uncomfortable ordeal. I'm sorry."

"Don't be. I'm just hoping you haven't had second thoughts about the feasibility of Dr. Maurois' theory working because it's too late now." She paused for breath. "I've set it in motion."

He braked at the entrance to the hospital parking area with enough force to rock the car. She felt those velvety brown depths impale her. "What are you saying?"

Hallie moistened her lips nervously. "Paul's going to get his wish. I'll be spending the summer at St. Genes."

Someone behind them was honking to get past. But a stillness had come over Vincent. She wondered if he was even aware of the other car. Finally he put down the window and motioned the driver to go around them.

"What about your plan to enter the convent?" There was a tone of incredulity in that low husky voice.

"It's been put on hold."

He remained motionless for another few seconds, then changed gears and made a right turn onto the boulevard.

A street lamp light glinted on the gold watch around his left wrist. It drew her attention to the tops of his strong, suntanned hands with their dusting of black hair. She noticed he wore no rings.

Her gaze took in the immaculate nails of his lean fingers. He handled the car with practiced ease. Fascinated by him, her eyes wandered over his well-honed physique. Every inch of it was hard-muscled sinew.

To her horror she found him so physically appealing, her palms grew clammy. After Raul, she hadn't thought she could feel feelings like this again.

Talk about human weakness—

"Paul understands I'll still be a lay nun, but he ran with his plans for me."

"I can imagine," Vincent murmured.

"He considers all his ideas a fait accompli. Before I left his room, I almost made the mistake of telling him he needed to get your approval first."

"We can thank heaven you didn't—" his voice shook "—otherwise he wouldn't be coming home. It's because of your sacrifice, Hallie. There are no words to express what I'm feeling right now."

She had no words, either.

A new fear had entered her heart. It had to do with the flesh and blood man seated next to her. A man she'd admired months before he'd exploded into her world one surreal night with all the fury of a comet hurtling from space.

CHAPTER FOUR

"PAPA? I'm back from the hospital!"

"One moment, Monique!" Vincent called to her. He was still on the phone with Dr. Maurois who was returning his call.

"Sorry for the interruption, Doctor."

"That's quite all right. I was just saying that since you're leaving for St. Genes in the morning, I'll have my secretary fax Paul's medical records to the hospital in Bordeaux.

"Dr. Cluny is an excellent psychiatrist. I'll consult with him so he's up to date on your son's case. If you have any questions, don't hesitate to call me."

"I won't."

Monique hurried into Vincent's bedroom. From the look on her face she was anxious to talk. He smiled at his daughter, pleased that things were better between the two of them.

"Before we hang up I wanted you to know today's visit with Ms. Linn was illuminating. More than ever I'm convinced this plan will work, probably sooner than we think.

"Consider it an encouraging sign that the initial crisis has passed without having to put Paul on heavy medication. In time you'll have your son back much better than before. I'm sure of it."

Vincent had little hope Paul would ever let him be a father to him again. The most he could expect would be a superficial civility, but he kept those thoughts to himself because his son was alive and looking forward to going home.

After the state he'd been in Thursday night, this much progress constituted a miracle. It was thanks to the selfless woman who was putting Paul's welfare ahead of her own needs and concerns.

"Thank you, Dr. Maurois. I'm very grateful. *Au revoir.*"

"Finally," Monique said as he clicked off. "Did you get hold of Monsieur Gide?"

While Vincent had finished up a lot of last minute phone calls in preparation for their flight to Bordeaux, Monique had spent all day with Paul before coming back to the apartment by taxi.

"I did. He'll put the check through tomorrow morning. Did Paul accept the ring?" Vincent had relied on Monique to know how to return it to her brother without upsetting him.

"Not at first." She sat down on the end of the bed. "But when I told him you said to give it back to him because it was his to deal with, he eventually reached for it."

"Thanks, petite. I can always count on you."

She eyed him with those soulful eyes. "Papa—if he tries to give it to Hallie again, I know she won't take it."

"How do you know that?"

"Because I just do."

Curious to find out what was going on in that razor-sharp mind of hers he said, "What's changed since Thursday when you willingly disappeared so he could ask her to marry him?"

She lowered her head. "Everything."

"He got what he wanted, didn't he? More time to

get to know her without fear of her leaving? I thought you were happy about that.''

"I am, but—"

"But what, *cherie?*"

"I don't know. Things just aren't the same now. Paul's different.''

The doctor had told Monique the truth about her brother's accident for her sake as well as Paul's. However he wisely didn't explain the reason behind Hallie's decision to come to St. Genes with them.

Monique was too close to Paul. In a moment of weakness she might confide something that would spell death to the doctor's strategy.

"In what way?"

"Well for one thing, I was in the room when he called the bank where he was supposed to have started training today. The manager bit his head off for wasting his time. Paul said some nasty things back before hanging up on him. He didn't even act like my brother.''

Dr. Maurois had said Paul needed to grow up and deal with the real world. Already his son was getting a taste of it.

"We're probably going to see Paul do a lot of things that seem out of character for a while. He's been through a life changing experience. All we can do is love him and be there for him.''

Tears rolled down her cheeks. "I wish none of this had happened.'' In the next breath she threw herself in his arms and cried.

Vincent had echoed those words the second he'd heard the jeweler talk about the beautiful aquamarine Paul had purchased for his intended. But oddly enough he didn't feel that way now.

There were things the twins didn't know. Secrets only

Pere Maurice was privy to. Secrets they had both sworn to take to the grave, believing it was for the best.

But the whole situation with Hallie had proved him wrong. The ring and the proposal, followed by Paul's accident, had brought Vincent out of a deep sleep.

Dr. Maurois didn't know it, but when he'd talked about the danger of Paul continuing to see the world through idealistic eyes, he could have been describing Vincent.

By living in denial about his past, Vincent was the one to blame for this crisis which had been coming on for a lifetime. No matter the consequences, his children needed to hear the truth to understand why he'd turned into a monster last Thursday night.

He was determined that once they were home again, he would sit them down and break his eighteen-year silence.

"Oh—" was all an enraptured Hallie could keep repeating as Vincent drove his luxury sedan past the gate marking the entrance to the Rolland estate. Rows and rows of healthy grape vines beneath a midafternoon sun paralleled the ribbon of road leading to the sprawling seventeenth century chateau in the distance.

Built on architectural lines that reminded her of the old French fairy tale of Cendrillon, the mellow yellow of the stones gleamed against all the greenery. She kept closing her eyes, then opening them again, for fear she was dreaming.

"It's real," Paul read her mind. The moment they'd deboarded the plane in Bordeaux, he'd followed her into the back seat of his father's car. "I told you it was beautiful."

Hallie shook her head, still in awe of such a glorious

sight. "No wonder you couldn't wait to return. This is paradise."

She was seated behind Vincent. Several times during the hour's drive from the airport their gazes had happened to meet in the rearview mirror. On the surface he appeared more relaxed, yet his eyes reflected a mixture of pain and some other dark emotion she couldn't decipher.

Suddenly Monique put down the window. "Pere!" she cried excitedly and started waving. "Let me out, Papa!"

Vincent slowed to a stop for his daughter. She opened the car door and hit the ground running. Hallie could see an old man and a dog in the courtyard.

"Beauregard!" Monique shouted to the spotted beagle who shot toward her so fast Hallie doubted his feet touched the ground. They met in a tangle of legs and fur.

Hallie's laughter turned to quiet tears as she witnessed the joyous reunion. By now Pere Maurice had joined them. They were all huddled together in one big embrace.

Vincent looked over his shoulder at his son. His eyes held signs of telltale moisture. "Would you like to get out and join them, or are you still too dizzy?"

"I told you I'm over that," he muttered without looking at Vincent. "I'll stay with Hallie till we reach the house."

She decided it was time he spent a few minutes alone with his father.

"Actually I'd like to get out and stretch my legs, Paul. I've never walked through a vineyard before."

Without waiting for a response, she opened her door and jumped down, closing it behind her. The air was soft and the blue sky was filled with patches of clouds, the kind you saw in a Manet painting.

She felt like she'd landed on the artist's canvas, the last dollop of paint. A dreary dollop at best in her white blouse and unremarkable gray skirt.

Instead of taking the road, she opted to walk between two rows of tall vines. The twins had taught her a lot about their vineyard. The soil was unusual for its iron-oxide, thus producing the merlot variety of grape. When they were ripe, they'd be harvested and turned into the famous Rolland wine which was more expensive than most due to its rarity.

To think Vincent had been born here, had worked the land and the vines with his father and grandfather before him. Such a unique heritage had turned out an extraordinary man in spite of the pain he'd been forced to suffer under a parent whose will had been law.

The beagle had seen her coming and raced over to investigate. She scratched behind his floppy ears. "Hello, Beauregard. You're even cuter than the twins said you were."

He licked her hands and ran around her legs while she covered the rest of the distance to the two people waiting for her.

The old Frenchman was as tall as Vincent, but a little stooped. He wore the typical brown beret on top of a surprisingly thick head of gray hair. His sweater hung loose on his lean figure.

Pere Maurice winked at her from the same dark brown eyes bequeathed to his family. Good looks ran in the Rolland gene pool.

"Beau likes you. See how his tail rotates."

It *did* rotate.

Both Monique and Hallie chuckled before she put out

her hand to shake his. "I'm so happy to meet you, Monsieur Rolland. The children have talked about you constantly."

His level gaze was friendly, yet he studied her as if she were a puzzle he was trying to solve. "Welcome to St. Genes, *mademoiselle.*"

"Since I'm going to be here for a while, please call me Hallie."

"Allie," he repeated.

"No, Pere. It's *H*allie. You have to say the h sound."

Hallie shook her head. "It doesn't matter, Monique. You can all call me whatever is easiest."

The old man nodded. "I like your attitude."

"I like being here."

She breathed in deeply and looked all around before her glance settled on Monique. "Do you remember the afternoon we went to see The Sound of Music with English subtitles?"

"Of course."

"Do you remember a line where Uncle Max said, 'Oh, I love being around rich people. I love how they live. I love how I live when I'm with them'?"

The French girl nodded and grinned.

"That's exactly how I feel right now."

The old man threw back his head and laughed, causing the dog to bark and do laps around their legs.

"What's so funny?" Vincent had approached them after parking the car. Paul trailed a little ways off.

Monique repeated the gist of their conversation.

"It's especially funny coming from the mouth of a nun," Pere Maurice quipped.

Vincent broke into the first full-bodied smile Hallie had seen. It transformed him. She thought her heart would never be the same again.

"Hallie's not a nun yet, Pere."

The brittle voice caused all of them to turn and look at Paul who stood just outside their circle.

Pere put a hand over his heart. "It's what's in here that counts, Paul."

Vincent's gaze met Hallie's for an instant, sending her a private message. His grandfather knew the score and was trying to help.

"How about a hug for your grandfather? It's been a long time. I've missed you."

Paul swallowed hard. "I've missed you, too." His gestures were wooden until his grandfather embraced him. Then Hallie saw his arms tighten around the old man's neck.

"Second in your class at the most difficult private school in Paris. I'm proud of you. This calls for a celebration."

"Monique came in first at hers."

"Only by three points," his sister inserted with commendable modesty.

Once again Hallie found herself the focus of Vincent's regard. He gave an imperceptible nod as if to say a little ground had been made. Paul was speaking to everyone again.

"Your Latin class was much harder than mine, Paul. If Hallie hadn't helped me understand the ablative case, I would have failed it."

Pere Maurice let go of Paul to tousle her dark curls. "The local priest used to teach us Latin. I can't say it did me much good."

Hallie smiled. "I wouldn't have taken it in high school if it hadn't been for my freshman English teacher. She said if you want to really understand

English or any of the Romance languages, you must take Latin. It turns out she was right.''

Paul looked completely bored with the conversation. "Come on, Hallie. I want to show you around the chateau.''

"I'd love a tour, but do you mind if I freshen up first?''

A dull red crept into his cheeks. "No. Of course not. I'll bring in your cases.''

"Better let Gaston do that, Paul. You're just out of the hospital.''

He glared at Pere. "I'm not an invalid.''

"You might be if you refuse to listen to reason. Come with me. I have something to show you.''

While he hesitated, Monique stood on tiptoe to kiss her father and Pere, then hooked her arm through Hallie's. "I'll take you to my room since you'll be sleeping there.''

"Only for a couple of nights,'' Paul reminded her. "Then she'll have her own room in one of the cottages. I phoned Bernard from Paris. He's already working on it.''

"I know,'' Monique murmured. "We'll meet you downstairs in a little while. Come along, Beau!'' They crossed the courtyard with the dog at their heels.

Hallie was glad to escape the tension. She didn't envy Vincent who'd been forced to walk on eggshells around his son since they'd picked him up at the hospital earlier in the day.

Pere was a different matter. He could say what needed to be said without fear of reprisal, but then he wasn't Paul's sworn enemy.

A shiver raced through Hallie's body.

"What's wrong?'' Monique was a quick study.

"How could anything be wrong in this beautiful place? To think you were born and raised here…"

"Be honest, Hallie. There's a lot wrong and we both know it," her companion lamented. "I know my brother's ill. The doctor told me. But it's hard to be around him when he's so mean."

"I know how you feel."

The French girl slowed her steps. "Hallie? Why did you really come?"

Hallie had been waiting for that question. She would tell her as much of the truth as she could.

"When I learned that Paul had run in front of that truck on purpose, I felt partially to blame. But the person carrying the biggest load of guilt is your father. He's so sorry for the way he acted. You can tell he's truly suffering, and that hurts me.

"I discussed it with Mother Marie-Claire. She agreed that I should put off my plans to go back to California in order to let your brother see I don't blame your father. Paul needs to understand that and forgive him or neither of them will be happy again.

"If there's anything I can do to help them get back together, I'll do it. Vin—your father—" she caught herself "—regrets the other night more than you'll ever know."

Monique stared at her for a long moment before nodding. By tacit agreement they entered the chateau where she was introduced to Etvige and her husband Gaston. The older housekeeper and her husband fussed over Monique like a pair of loving grandparents.

Beauregard kept barking from the steps of the magnificent curving staircase ahead of them, totally unaware that not all creatures great or small could call such a place home.

Hallie had been to Versailles and the Chateaux Country with the twins since coming to France. All of them were magnificent in their own way. But this chateau was the most special of all because the Rolland family lived here.

Vincent lived here.

As she stood on the inlaid parquetry staggered by feelings just the thought of him engendered, she could hear Monique's question resounding in her head.

Hallie? Why did you really come?

Hallie hoped it was for the reason she'd given her, *and* because she wanted Dr. Maurois's theory to work.

But what if there was more to it than that?

What if Vincent himself was part of the reason?

What if she'd come because...

No.

She couldn't think that way. She daren't think it.

"Hallie?"

Monique's voice jerked her from her torturous thoughts.

"Sorry I'm a slowpoke. There's so much to look at, I'm dazzled."

She caught up to her on the next floor. Monique explained her suite of rooms was to the left of the staircase. Her father's and Paul's were to the right. Pere's was on the main floor so he wouldn't have to climb stairs.

Besides a huge blue and white bedroom with two big beds and a fireplace, she had a large bathroom which had been modernized, and her own sitting room made up as a study with a computer.

"This suite is bigger than most people's homes," Hallie said when she emerged from the bathroom a few minutes later.

"That's what my friends say when they stay over-night. I've had huge parties in here. Everyone brings a sleeping bag. It was hard getting used to the tiny rooms at school in Paris. I love my space."

By now Monique was sitting in the middle of her bed, hugging a pillow to her chest. The dog had climbed up on top with her. He'd found a toy and they were playing tug of war.

Hallie wandered over to one of the windows. The view of the vineyards was a sight she could look at forever. Out of the corner of her eye she saw Paul and Pere walking toward a cluster of outbuildings.

There was no sign of Vincent.

Her heart ached for him. He'd been waiting for the twins' homecoming, only to have it turn into a night-mare that could last for a long time.

In the midst of her thoughts she heard the phone ring. When she turned around, Monique was reaching for it at the side of the bed. As soon as she cried, "Suzette!" Hallie knew it would be a while before Monique was free.

Suzette was her best friend in St. Genes. They'd emailed each other constantly to stay in touch. Monique needed her right now. Paul needed to be with his good friends, too.

Mouthing the words that she'd be downstairs, Hallie left the bedroom with the intention of doing some ex-ploring. But she only made it as far as the grand stair-case when she saw Vincent coming up the marble steps.

He took them two at a time with a careless male grace that was poetry to watch. When he saw her standing at the top, he slowed down.

"Hallie—"

Through narrowed lids his eyes seemed to take in-

ventory of her face and figure. Perhaps it was because
he hadn't expected to see her standing there that he'd
been caught off guard. Whatever the reason, the inti-
macy of his perusal set her trembling.

"Monique's on the phone with Suzette so I thought
I'd look around for a little while," she said, hoping she
didn't sound nervous. "Would that be all right?"

"Of course. While you're here I want you to treat
this place as your home." He rubbed his chest absently,
a gesture she'd seen him do before when he was con-
templating something serious. "However as long as
we're alone for the moment, there's something important I need to discuss with you."

She felt her heart thud with anxiety. "Did you and
Paul have words after I got out of the car?"

His features darkened. "No. There was total silence
which was much worse."

She bit her lip. "This has to be so hard on you."

He nodded. "We can't talk here. Come with me."

As before, he cupped her elbow and guided her down
the hall past several rooms to another set of tall French
doors. They opened into an alcove that led to a sitting
room of sorts.

It contained love seats, couches and half a dozen
paintings of the estate obviously done at different per-
iods dating from the 1700s.

There was another painting too that drew Hallie's interest. It depicted a tall, thin, unsmiling nobleman with
dark hair and eyes like slits. The engraved brass plaque
read Le Duc de Rolland.

"Monique thinks he's scary looking," said a deep
voice behind her. "We keep him in here rather than the
library downstairs so he doesn't terrify our guests."

A gentle chuckle escaped Hallie's throat.

"From all accounts he was a scary man. I think my father must have inherited some of his genes," his voice grated. "After Thursday night I'm sure my children are saying the same thing about me."

Her smile vanished.

It was no accident he'd brought her to this room.

Hallie spun around. "What did your father do that has caused you to carry such a heavy weight all these years?"

His head was bowed so she couldn't see the torment on his face, but it was there in his ragged voice. "My father was difficult, but he wasn't to blame for the mistakes I made. Those were mine alone."

She moved closer. "What mistakes?"

CHAPTER FIVE

"WHEN I walked in on you and Paul, it was as if the years had just rolled away and I was seventeen again, almost Paul's age.

"I saw myself in the cottage bedroom of one of our winery workers. The champagne bottle and glasses were familiar. Instead of a three carat aquamarine ring worth nine thousand dollars, a dazzling pair of diamond earrings worth five thousand dollars I'd borrowed against a plot of land adorned the ears of my beloved."

Oh no. Hallie's hand dug into the armrest of the love seat.

"The only difference was that the female in my arms was an impossibly beautiful witch with hair black as midnight rather than your spun gold silk. Arlette was nine years my senior, only a year older than you are now."

Hallie could appreciate the similarities like no one else.

"She was barely widowed due to her husband's fatal heart attack."

Raul hadn't been gone that long, either. The similarities were growing more remarkable by the second.

"Arlette's interest flattered a boy like me who'd just started to test the waters. When she invited me to go swimming with her one afternoon, her passionate response to my clumsy, untutored lovemaking held me enthralled."

Hallie lowered her head, trying to fight the images his words conjured.

"When I saw other men hanging around her, watching her during the day, my jealousy became uncontrollable. For six months or more I sold my soul to be in her arms and her bed. There wasn't enough I could do to prove my devotion.

"Besides the diamonds, I gave her money to pay the rent on the cottage so she could stay on the estate. In time I was totally supporting her. All interest in my schoolwork, the family business, paled into insignificance beside her enslaving charms."

Paul's words rang in Hallie's ears. *You don't have to work. I'll support you.*

Vincent took a shuddering breath and lifted his head. Hallie listened in shocked fascination as he continued to bare his soul.

"I would slip away from the chateau after dark to be with her. I believed I was so clever, no one knew about my nocturnal visits. After all, my father's health was failing from liver disease. My grandfather was in his own world, grieving for my grandmother who'd died of pneumonia."

Paul had kept Hallie a secret from his father. Loyal Monique had gone along with her brother because she loved him.

"Every day was exciting because I knew that every night I'd be with Arlette. It wasn't until my father was close to death that I found out he'd known all along about our affair. He warned me she was only after the Rolland fortune, that I must give her up.

"I thought the things he'd said were the ravings of a man who'd never known how to be happy and didn't want me to be happy, either. A few weeks later he surprised me when his dying words asked me to for-give him.

"Soon after the funeral I made plans to marry Arlette, but the priest ran to Pere Maurice who stopped the cer-emony before it could take place.

"To my shock, my grandfather who'd always been there to make things better for me, didn't pull through this time. Instead he reiterated everything my father had said about Arlette and much more.

"Apparently he'd found out she'd run away from home at an early age and had been with more men than he could count. After telling me she wasn't worthy to kiss the ground I walked on, he forbid me to see her anymore or he would disown me.

"At that point in time I didn't give a damn about her past or my heritage. All I wanted was Arlette. When I told her we were going away to run away and get mar-ried, that I'd find a job somewhere else, she informed me she was pregnant.

"You can't imagine my joy. I felt as if Pere Noel had delivered all the Christmas toys at my door. Now we would have to get married and it would be with Pere Maurice's blessing. With a great grandchild on the way, he would want to be involved in its life.

"So the priest ended up performing our nuptials, but my happiness didn't last long. I won't burden you with the sordid details. Needless to say she no longer wel-comed me in bed.

"For a time I thought it was because she had morning sickness. But I soon learned she'd been leaving the cha-teau during the day to be with other men."

The reason for Vincent's rage was no longer a mys-tery.

"When I confronted her, she admitted she'd only

used a pathetic boy like me to get what she wanted. From then on we had long, nightmarish quarrels. I came close to leaving her on one occasion when she threw it in my face that she'd never been attracted to me and had only married me for my money. I threatened to cut off her funds. She threatened to abort our child.''

"Vincent—'' Hallie murmured in pain. ''I can see why you thought I might be pregnant.'' It all made perfect sense.

He stared hard at her. "Except I didn't know I was confronting an angel of mercy instead of a loose, opportunistic woman like Arlette.''

I'm no angel, Vincent. Anything but.

His eyes closed for a moment. "I almost lost my sanity because by then the baby had come to mean everything to me. It represented the only good, pure, undefiled thing in our doomed travesty of a marriage.

"In order to prevent her from killing our child, I was so desperate I went to Pere. He took pity on me. Together we went to our family attorney who drew up a legal document stating that my inheritance from the vineyards would revert to her the moment the baby was born.

"Conversely, as soon as she was well enough to go home from the hospital, she would have to leave the estate and never attempt to see me or the baby again.''

"And she agreed to that?'' Hallie was aghast.

"Oh yes. She agreed with an avaricious eagerness that killed every last particle of tenderness or feeling I might have harbored in the deepest recess of my soul for her.

"After she delivered twins, she couldn't leave the hospital fast enough. She never once held either of them in her arms.''

Hallie shook her head in confusion. "But the twins told me she died in childbirth."

His brooding gaze switched to her. "That's what I wanted them to believe."

She sucked in her breath. "I—is she still alive?"

"No, *grace a dieu*."

"Then I don't understand."

"Less than a year later I found out through our attorney that she'd spent all my family's money and had been killed in a tram accident in Cortina with her latest lover.

"I received the news with unholy joy knowing she could never renege on her word or hurt the children. I started to come back to the world of the living after that."

Hallie stared at him. "You were so young to have gone through such a heartbreaking experience. I can't imagine it."

"Don't feel bad for me. Even though I'd brought everything on myself, I got the help I needed. Pere had no particular fondness for me at that point, but it was love at first sight when he held Paul and Monique in his arms."

Tears spilled over her lashes picturing them with the babies.

"We'd sold off half the vineyards to pay Arlette, but we still had the other half and the chateau. Between the two of us we managed to raise the children and run the business.

"Pere took turns with me playing nursemaid so I could attend classes at the university in Bordeaux. Once I received my business degree, I worked night and day to make the winery prosper. Slowly we recouped our earlier losses and I concentrated on being the best father I could.

"I decided that when the children were old enough to ask about their mother, I would tell them they were conceived in love, but that she'd died before she could raise them. I didn't want their lives scarred or diminished in any way by hearing the truth."

Hallie wiped the moisture from her cheeks. It was a tragic story.

His expression softened when he saw her wet face. "It happened over eighteen years ago, Hallie. The three of us have had a wonderful life together since then."

"Until last Thursday you mean. I should never have let Monique talk me into going to your apartment. But I loved being with them so much, I thought one last time wouldn't hurt."

Vincent shook his head. "It wouldn't have been the last time. I know my son. He would have followed you to California. As it is, he found a very dramatic way to get you here to St. Genes."

He was right about that.

Hallie rose to her feet. "You have to tell the twins what you told me."

"I'm planning to, but I wanted your approval first."

"You have it," she blurted emotionally. "When they hear your story, they'll understand everything. Paul will realize you were trying to prevent history from repeating itself, and he'll forgive you. So will Monique."

"You mean the truth will make them free?"

"Yes."

"Free maybe to hate me for the lie I've allowed them to go on believing about their mother all these years."

"Then they'll have to hate Pere Maurice, too. He has perpetuated the lie."

"Pere is a saint. However if I've learned anything from this experience, it's that I haven't done any favors for my children by trying to make a perfect world for them.

"Paul believes that if he wants something, just wishing for it will make it so. He's so much like I was at his age, it's uncanny."

Her eyes searched his. "Perhaps that's why your father asked for your forgiveness. He probably realized the damage he'd done by keeping you too tied to him. If he'd given you some freedom, you would have lived a more normal life like your friends.

"Then again, you would never have had Paul and Monique. I can't imagine this world without them."

"Neither can I," he said in a husky voice.

She slid her hands in the pockets of her skirt. "When are you going to tell them?"

"I was thinking this evening after dinner."

"I'm glad."

"I figure I'm already in the doghouse. If there's to be a chance of this family really healing, I might as well get everything out in the open now."

Hallie's admiration for him was growing in quantum leaps. "I want to help. Tell me—does your grandfather play board games like chess?"

His raised his eyebrows. "Yes. That's one of his favorites. Why?"

"While we're eating dinner, I'll suggest we have a match afterward. It will thwart Paul in case he wants to go for a walk with me or something. That way he'll be free to join you and Monique for your chat."

She saw something flicker in the dark depths of his eyes. "It's a perfe—"

"Papa?" Monique's voice caused both their heads to

turn. "Where are you? Papa?" It sounded like she was right outside the doors to the room.

"I'm coming, *petite!*" He turned to Hallie. "Shall we go?"

She did his bidding and followed him to the corridor. But the second she saw the curious look Monique gave them, she experienced the oddest sensation. It was like the way you felt when you'd been caught doing something wrong.

If Vincent felt it, too, he gave no indication as he reached for his daughter and hugged her. "Do you have any idea how wonderful it is to hear your voice in this hallway again? How does it feel to be home?"

"I love it."

"What does Suzette have to say for herself?"

Hallie bent down and gave Beauregard a good rub before following them to the stairs. He supplied the welcome diversion she needed right then.

"There you are," Paul exclaimed after coming out of Monique's room. "I've been looking all over for you, Hallie."

Guilt swamped her again.

"Your father was showing me the famous Duc de Rolland painting. You two told me your family descended from royalty, but I pictured someone quite different."

They started down the steps.

"The man is hideous," Monique declared over her shoulder. "I can't believe he's our relative."

Her father chuckled, but there wasn't as much as a muscle twitch from Paul.

Etvige met them in the foyer and told them Minou had dinner ready in the small dining room. "She has prepared your favorite escalope de veau and plum cake for dessert, *mes enfants*."

"I've been waiting nine months for this!" Monique cried. "You're going to love her cooking, Hallie. No one makes bread like Minou. Wait until you bite into one of her baguettes fresh from the oven. Oh la la."

A half hour later Hallie realized Monique hadn't been exaggerating about Minou's cooking. She'd never eaten a more delicious meal. Though Paul remained taciturn, Monique entertained everyone with stories about her school adventures.

They were approaching the much anticipated plum cake when Paul had visitors. Etvige showed them into the dining room. Word had spread that the Rollands were home from Paris. Two of his best friends from St. Genes had come over on their motor scooters eager for him to go for a ride with them.

Vincent urged them to sit down first and have some cake. They thanked him, said hi to Monique and took their places at the table.

Paul looked anything but pleased, so his father covered for his lack of manners and made the introductions. "Jules? Luc? Meet Hallie Linn. She's a friend of the twins from Paris."

The typical looking French teenagers with their T-shirts and leather jackets were a gregarious couple of guys. If they noticed Paul wasn't saying anything, it didn't seem to bother them.

Luc enjoyed teasing Monique who gave as good as she got. Jules, to Hallie's consternation, kept plying her with questions and at one point suggested that if she didn't have anything else to do, she should come with them for the evening.

Paul protested. "I'm planning to show her the cottage I'm getting ready for her. Maybe another night, guys."

"That's okay, Paul," Hallie said. "We can do it tomorrow when your friends aren't here. Actually tonight I was hoping Pere would teach me a few fundamentals of chess. I'm trying to learn the game and hear he's an expert."

The old man's eyes twinkled. "I'd be delighted. You go on and enjoy yourself with Luc and Jules, Paul."

Her gaze met Vincent's before it shifted to his grandfather. "It may not be that fun for you. I'm pretty dense when it comes to games of strategy, but it's a skill I'd like to acquire."

Minou chose that moment to bring in second helpings of cake which the boys devoured. The minute they'd finished, Paul got up from the table and the three of them disappeared from the dining room.

"Come on, petite," their father said. "Let's go upstairs to my room. There's something I want to talk to you about."

Pere rose more slowly. "Stay put, 'Allie. I'll get my chess set and be right back."

"I'll be waiting."

Vincent put a hand on his grandfather's shoulder. "Something tells me she knows more about the game than she's telling."

"Hmph."

Hallie's lips curved, but she didn't dare look at her host right then. Even if he would have to find another time to talk to Paul, he intended to unburden himself to his daughter tonight. It was the right thing to do, but she was still nervous for him.

Monique made the little goodbye motion with her fingers that was her trademark. "See you later, Hallie."

She made the same gesture back. While she was sitting there alone she heard voices in the hall. It seemed Paul had decided not to go with his friends after all. When he didn't come straight back to the dining room, it meant his father's wish to talk to him had prevailed.

Hallie hoped that was the case. It would be better if Vincent were able to tell the twins together.

While she was saying a silent prayer that all would go well, Pere returned with his game. The old man was brilliant at chess and a real joy to be around. He explained his strategy on several moves so she could learn. Near eleven they called it a night and planned to continue their match the next evening.

"Hallie? Are you asleep?"

The clock said three in the morning. Hallie had been waiting hours for Monique to come to bed. But she didn't want the other girl to know she'd been counting them, or that she'd been worrying herself sick over the twins' reactions.

"I'm not now," she answered in a purposely wry tone. Twisting around, she sat up to turn on the lamp next to her bed.

Monique had slipped on a long flowing nightgown. Her complexion looked blotchy, the telltale sign of a long crying spell.

"I'm sorry, but I need to talk to you."

"Come on then. Sit on my bed."

Hallie sat against the headboard with her knees raised beneath the covers.

"What's happened?"

"Tonight Papa told me and Paul about his life growing up, about his father and...our mother."

Hallie held her breath wondering what was coming next.

"He said he's already told you everything because you deserved to understand why he was so cruel to you at the apartment."

"Your father's an amazing man. It took a lot of courage for him to talk about the past when it was so painful."

Monique bowed her head. "I always wondered why he didn't get married again. But I was happy he never did because I didn't want our family to change. I wish—I wish I didn't know all those things." Her voice trembled.

Hallie's heart went out to her. She wanted to put her arms around her and comfort her. Instead she hooked her arms around her own knees. "What upsets you most?"

After the question had hung in the air for a minute Monique said, "That I might turn out to be like her."

Another prayer had been answered. Monique hadn't turned on her father.

"You should be proud that you inherited her best qualities and beauty, the things she was born with that attracted your father. Never forget that when he first met her, he *did* love her with all his heart. That's important for you to know.

"But Monique—you couldn't have inherited her unhappy upbringing. A child has to be taught correct principles. Something went wrong in her own family for her to run away from home. That's why she turned into the person she became.

"It's very evident she didn't have a parent like your father to guide her."

"There's nobody like Papa."

"I agree. And when you really think about it, your father's father—no matter how strict and unyielding he

was—had to have done a lot of things right to turn out
a son as fine as your father. You and Paul received the
kind of love from him every child deserves, and it
shows!

"You're both so exceptional, that as we say in
America, you stood out a mile from your other friends
when I met you in Paris. You made me love you when
I shouldn't have." Her voice caught.

Silence filled the room like a fine mist.

"Thank you, Hallie," she cried softly. "I love you,
too."

Before she knew it, they were hugging.

Finally Monique moved to her own bed. Hallie turned
off the light before sliding beneath the covers, confident
Monique was going to be fine.

But when Hallie thought about Vincent's state of
mind, she realized she would never go to sleep.

Paul was out there somewhere. Who knew what condition he was in after hearing the truth about his mother.

Hallie turned her face into the pillow and wept.

Vincent gave up trying to sleep for what was left of the
rest of the night. He levered himself from the bed for a
shower and shave. By the time he'd dressed in a sport
shirt and jeans, it was quarter to seven.

He headed downstairs, hoping Hallie was up. They
needed to have another talk about his son who'd had
plenty of alarming things to say to him after Monique
had left his bedroom last night. Normally it was his
daughter who was the most talkative on a subject at any
given time.

Not last night. When she'd finally slipped from the
room like a wraith, he felt as if a giant hand were
squeezing the blood from his heart.

Prepared to answer any questions about their mother so no stone would be left unturned, Vincent received his second shock of the night when it was Hallie his angry son wanted to talk about.

"I'm sorry things didn't work out for you and my mother, but I don't know why you had to lie about it."

"Obviously I was trying to protect you."

"I don't need you to protect me. A lot of guys at my school in Paris have similar stories. Even Luc's mom did the same thing to his dad. It happens."

He shrugged his shoulders with a nonchalance that was stunning for Vincent to watch.

"The point is, Hallie's nothing like my mother. I know she's older than I am, but it doesn't bother me, and the age difference between you and my mother sure as hell never bothered *you*."

Paul had picked up quite a mouth at boarding school along with a large dose of unattractive cynicism.

"Another thing about Hallie. She's been married before, and she was happy!"

That was a bombshell Vincent hadn't been expecting.

If Monique had known about it, she'd never confided it to him. Why it mattered to Vincent he didn't know, but the news left him oddly disturbed.

"She would still be married to him if he hadn't died, so you can forget that she suddenly decided she wanted to sleep with someone else."

The blows kept coming.

"Right now Hallie doesn't know what she wants and is honest enough to admit it. That's why she came to St. Genes. She has grown to love me. It's not the way she loved her husband. But I can wait until she stops seeing him everywhere, and starts seeing me.

"Hallie became a lay nun as a way to get over her

pain by serving others.'' He squinted hard at Vincent. "She doesn't sound a lot like my mother does she,'' came the sarcastic remark.

Paul would never forgive him for his attack on Hallie's character.

"I'm just thankful she turned to God, otherwise I wouldn't have met her. But I can promise you this—she was never meant to be a nun, and I'm going to prove it!''

For punctuation he'd slammed Vincent's bedroom door.

"Etvige?'' When Vincent couldn't find anyone in the dining room, he'd walked through to the kitchen. "Have you seen Hallie?''

"*Oui*. She left for town a half hour ago.''

He frowned. "Alone?''

"Yes.''

"Did Gaston drive her?''

"No. She said it was such a beautiful morning, she wanted to walk.''

A spurt of adrenaline charged his body.

"Have either of the twins been down yet?''

"Pas encore. Are you ready for your coffee and rolls?''

"Not this morning. I have business in Libourne. Tell the twins I'll be back for lunch.''

"Will do.''

A few minutes later he glimpsed a blond-haired woman in the distance. He pulled his car behind her. She was walking in sneakers at a brisk clip. With head held high she crossed the stone bridge leading into the medieval town.

She'd thrown a thin cardigan sweater over her simple blouse and skirt. Yet like a magnet his gaze was drawn to her voluptuous figure and long legs, the kind he admired on American women.

Vincent had never coveted another man's wife, but he found himself envying the man who'd had the right to be with her day and night. The husband who'd known her in *every* sense...

The revelation that she'd been married before joining her order as a lay nun changed the way he thought of Hallie.

Until Paul had said anything, Vincent supposed his mind had put both of them in some nebulous category labeled innocent.

Nothing could be further from the truth. Not in Hallie's case, and possibly not in Paul's.

His son had been dating girls since he'd turned sixteen, but as far as Vincent knew there hadn't been anyone special. However that didn't mean Paul hadn't experimented with a local girl before he'd left for Paris.

He hoped he hadn't.

They'd had long talks about the dangers of getting physically involved too young, not to mention the moral issue. Vincent had given Monique the same talks. He assumed she was still a virgin, but what did a parent really know.

Not much when he recalled his shock upon hearing that his son had bought a nine thousand dollar engagement ring for Hallie.

Paul loved her.

He desired her.

When Vincent realized how far he'd allowed his own intimate thoughts of Hallie to intrude on his consciousness, he felt sick to the pit of his stomach.

"Vincent?"

At the sound of her voice he came back to a cognizance of his surroundings. She must have sensed a car behind her because she'd stopped on the other side of the bridge to let him pass.

He pulled in front of her and stopped.

She walked up to the passenger side and opened the door. "Were you looking for me?"

Her question threw him into a moral quandary. Should he lie and tell her no because he knew it would be wrong to spend any more time alone with her?

Then she leaned inside, and he found he had no defense against a pair of flawless aqua eyes staring at him with anxiety.

"Yes," he said in a thick-tone voice. "I was hoping I might find you downstairs, but Etvige said you'd left the chateau."

"I decided to go to church before I did anything else."

Maybe that was what he needed.

"Do you mind if we take a drive first so we can talk, then I'll go to church with you."

He thought he detected the slightest hesitation before she murmured her assent. As soon as she got in the car, he turned it around and drove back over the bridge.

"There's a place on our property near the Dordogne river you ought to see while you're here."

He took the next left onto a single lane road. After following it through the lush countryside to a cherished spot, he stopped the car. From this view you could see the elbow in the river.

Rows of grape vines met the water. Though there was a swift current, the top looked like glass. The rounded shapes of the trees matched the same cloud formations in the sky.

He cast her a covert glance, eager to witness her reaction. Again he had to ask himself why he wanted her to see what *he* saw in the view.

"It's so beautiful." Her breath caught. "It couldn't be real. It just couldn't." Her dazed eyes swerved to his. "Is this whe—"

"No—we never came here, it's too deep and dangerous."

"I wasn't going to bring up Arlette," she assured him quietly. "I wouldn't be that insensitive. I thought maybe this was your favorite swimming hole growing up with your friends."

Mon Dieu, what was wrong with him?

"I'm sorry, Hallie. The last thing I want to do is offend you. Now that the twins know about their mother, I want to close the door on that chapter of our lives forever."

"I don't blame you."

"But will you be able to forgive me?"

She jerked her head around. He saw a blur of blue-green fire. "How can you ask me that? Don't you realize I'm your friend?"

Friend.

In his gut he recognized he wanted her to be more than that to him. He wanted...

"Tell me what Paul's reaction was like. Does he wish you hadn't destroyed his image of his mother?"

He struggled for breath. "Paul took the news much better than I would have imagined."

"So did Monique. Her last words before she went to sleep were, 'There's no one like Papa.'"

Vincent felt his eyes smart. "Thank you for telling me that. I just wish the rest of it were as simple." His hand curled tighter around the steering wheel.

Her expression fell. "I don't understand. I thought

you inferred Paul had forgiven you and is talking to you again. What's wrong now?''

''It's true we've reached a place where he's at least acknowledging my existence. Unfortunately I'm afraid we're going to have to scratch Dr. Maurois's theory and come up with a new plan.''

''Why?''

''A new ingredient has slipped into the mix neither I nor the good doctor knew about when we talked at the hospital.''

Her eyes implored him to be specific.

''Your previous marriage,'' he muttered.

She lowered her head.

Since meeting Hallie, one of the things he'd found remarkable about her was her outward calm. To watch her unexpectedly clasp her fingers until they went white revealed she was barely holding on to her control.

Vincent knew all about that chaotic state.

For some inexplicable reason he liked the idea that she could be thrown off base as well.

''Now that Paul knows you've been a woman in every sense of the word, he's convinced you're not nun material. On the contrary, he finds your interests and needs an irresistible challenge rather than a turnoff.

''Before he left my room he made it clear he intends to become so important to you, you won't look at him and see your husband's face anymore. You'll see Paul's.''

CHAPTER SIX

WHAT a bitter irony that Paul was hoping in vain for something that would never happen. Never *could* happen.

Not when it was his father's arresting face Hallie was starting to see every night in her dreams. It was Vincent's deep compelling voice she listened for on the stairs; his tangy masculine scent she detected when he'd just come from the shower; his electrifying touch on her arm sending curling warmth through her body.

Hallie didn't dare think about the way his mouth would taste and feel or she'd go mad. She had to get out of the car. It was impossible to concentrate on anything with him sitting so close to her.

Once free of the sedan's confines, she wandered to the river's edge.

It had taken a year after Raul's death before it began to alarm her that she couldn't recall his face clearly. When coupled with her loss, this brought on a terrible sadness that had driven her to talk to Gaby.

Her roommate had been the right person in whom to confide. She'd also lost a husband who'd died in a freak boating accident.

Gaby had told Hallie the cycle of denial, anger, pain and guilt she was experiencing was normal. She'd been through all the phases herself and had survived.

Being the great friend she was, she assured Hallie this period would pass. In time she would work through her travail and find peace again.

Those words had turned out to be prophetic.

Hallie did find her plateau of serenity. Through service to others, life held purpose once more. But that serenity had been threatened since she'd met Vincent Rolland.

She heard footsteps behind her. "Hallie?" His voice had a gravelly sound.

Afraid to be alone with him any longer she said, "Would you drive me to the church now?"

After a tension-filled pause, "Of course."

During the ride back to town she refused to look at him. To her relief he didn't try to talk to her.

When he'd parked the car, her emotions were in such havoc she couldn't appreciate the beauty of the centuries old building. Without waiting to see what he would do, she entered the church foyer.

An old woman with a scarf around her head was just coming out the doors. Hallie approached her.

"Excuse me. Could you tell me where I could find the priest?"

Her pale eyes widened in surprise. "Around the corner. His office is on the right."

"Thank you."

Hallie found it without problem. She knocked and was told to wait. A few minutes later a young couple came out and the priest signaled Hallie to enter. He looked close in age to Pere Maurice.

After introducing herself, she explained she was a lay nun from Paris serving in the area. Father Olivier gave her a cordial welcome. When she told him she was living on the Rolland estate, he beamed in delight. It seemed he held the entire family in great respect, particularly Pere who was an old friend.

"Father? I'd like to be of service while I'm here. In

the hallway I noticed a list of summer programs for the young people in the area. Do you think some of them might like help with their English?''

''That would be wonderful. Tourism is important here. Our teens always want assistance to get better paying jobs. Why don't you come to the youth group on Thursday at seven. I'll introduce you and we'll go from there.''

''Thank you, Father.''

He accompanied her to the door of his office. ''Tell Maurice I'll call around on the weekend for a visit.''

''I will.''

Walking with a little lighter step, she went into the church through a side door to pray. When she got up to leave, she discovered Vincent sitting in the last pew waiting for her.

She'd been all right until she'd seen him. Whether awake, asleep, or at prayer, he seemed to be there in the background of her life. It stirred up her emotions all over again.

Once they were back in the car, she felt compelled to finish the conversation they'd started at the river.

''At the hospital I told Paul I'd been married before. I said it in the hope he wouldn't see me as some kind of saint. In some small way I feared that was part of his attraction to me. It was a case of trying to take the bloom off the rose.''

The man at her side made a strange sound in his throat. ''Now you know differently. He sees you as an attainable woman.''

She stared out the window, blind to the passing landscape. ''I'd leave St. Genes today if the situation weren't so precarious. As it is, I put him off twice yesterday. He's not going to like it that I left this morni—''

Hallie stopped midsentence because they both saw Paul at the same time. He was coming toward them riding his two-seater motor scooter.

"I'll handle this."

Vincent slowed to a stop at the side of the road. He got out of the car as Paul made a U-turn and pulled up behind them.

Hallie couldn't sit there and not do something. Last night Vincent had started to make a little headway with Paul in their personal relationship. If Paul felt she and his father were going behind his back for any reason, he would blame Vincent. She couldn't let that happen.

"*Bonjour,*" she said after alighting from the car.

Paul's dour expression didn't bode well for the day. "I thought you would sleep in."

"That's a luxury for youth," she remarked deliberately. "When you're a few years older you'll find you wake up early no matter what."

"She's right," Vincent concurred. "Enjoy it while you can."

"I would have gotten up."

"As I recall, neither you or Monique are crazy about attending church at seven in the morning."

The harsh lines creasing his face relaxed somewhat. "Where are you going now?"

"Back to the chateau," Vincent answered for her. "I saw Hallie on the bridge and offered her a ride."

He'd said exactly what she was going to say.

"I'll take you," he offered.

"Have you forgotten the rules I have to follow? No swimming, no dancing, no inappropriate music, no riding pillion on horse or motorbike."

Paul frowned. "That was when you were in Paris."

She shook her head. "It applies anywhere I go while I'm part of the outreach program."

He obviously didn't want to be reminded of that, but he couldn't argue the point.

"I wanted to show you around."

"Tell you what," Vincent inserted. "I've finished my business for the day." At that remark Hallie averted her eyes. "You take our guest in the car, and I'll go home on your scooter." He handed Paul the keys.

Vincent's solution to the latest crisis reminded her that if Paul hadn't bought her that ring, he and Monique would have a car of their own right now.

"Thanks," Paul muttered.

His father couldn't have said or done anything to please his son more.

When she'd first seen Paul coming around the bend in the road, she'd feared the worst.

"You're welcome."

Hallie folded her arms. "How long has it been since you rode one of these things?" She couldn't help smiling at Vincent who was now seated astride it.

He looked at Paul. "When did we test this model out at the store?"

"Two years ago."

"Isn't there a law about you wearing a helmet when you ride?"

"Around here?" Paul sounded incredulous. "It's a scooter, not a motorbike!"

She raised her eyebrows. "Nevertheless most accidents happen within three miles of home."

Paul made a sound of protest. "You sound as bad as Jules's mother."

For a split second she and Vincent exchanged amused glances before he said, "I promise to be careful."

He started it up and took off smoothly. For a tall, powerfully built man, Vincent had a natural athletic grace that stood out from other men. No one observing him would know he hadn't been riding it every day.

Hallie shielded her eyes from the sun to watch him go. When he disappeared around the bend, her sense of loss grew acute. She hurried back to the car, hoping Paul would never pick up on her unwitting attraction to his father.

"What would you like to do on your first day here?" He'd turned on the ignition and was ready to get started.

She combed fingers through her hair to hide her trembling. "Could we drive to St. Emilion to see the cathedral and catacombs? Monique mentioned something about a monk who lived in a cave back in the eighth century. I believe she talked about a monolithic church carved out of the rock?"

Her suggestion met with a glower. "You've already been to church this morning."

"I can't ever get too much of it."

"You're in wine country now, Hallie. I'd like to take you to some caves where you can taste the different varieties."

"I know you would, but I don't drink alcohol so the experience would be wasted on me."

"Is that one of the order's rules, too?" came the petulant sounding question.

"No. Personal preference. I got so sick on margaritas during a high school trip to Mexico, I couldn't eat for several days. It ruined my whole vacation. I haven't gone near alcohol since."

"Hadn't you ever tasted it before?"

"No. Unlike your experience, my father didn't put wine in my water from the time I was old enough to sit at the table. That's probably the reason why I didn't know when to stop after I finally got the chance to try it."

"I can't picture you drunk."

"I don't want to remember it, believe me. However such a bad experience didn't stop me from marveling over the dozens of vineyards we saw on our drive from Bordeaux yesterday. I would imagine working in your father's winery office will teach me a lot.

"In fact that reminds me we'd better visit the manager as soon as we get back from St. Emilion. Mother Marie-Claire is expecting a fax from Monsieur Brouard verifying my employment. The sooner she can apply for an extension of my work visa, the better."

A frustrated sigh came from his side of the car. "Let's go see Yves now and get it over with. I'll show you the cottage, too."

He waited for several cars to pass, then pulled onto the road. "Afterward we can spend as long as we want in St. Emilion. There's a restaurant on the hill where we can have dinner. You'll love the view."

"Great as that sounds, I think we'll have to do that another time."

"Why?"

"Tonight Pere Maurice wants to test me out on what he taught me. I'd hate to disappoint him. What about your summer job? How soon are you going to start?"

"I don't know." Color seeped into his cheeks. "I just got home. Give me a little time—"

He pounded his fist gently against the steering wheel.

"Sorry, Hallie. I didn't mean to come off sounding rude."

"I'm sorry if I made you feel defensive."

She waited for him to reassure her she'd done nothing

wrong. When no words were forthcoming, she began to believe Dr. Maurois's idea was working.

This was the first time Paul had ever been prickly with her. Though he would never admit it, her actions had begun to irritate him. They acted like roadblocks.

If she continued to stay busy with her own agenda, it would create more disenchantment until he eventually gave up on her. Thankfully when that moment came, he wouldn't be able to blame his father.

Somewhat encouraged, she looked forward to getting settled in her new job. Gaby had called work the great panacea. Hallie could only echo her words.

While she tried to put thoughts of Vincent out of her mind, Paul drove her to the winery office in one of the outbuildings behind the chateau. The other buildings comprised the cottages.

Their exteriors matched the chateau's style and were deceptive. Inside she discovered a modern office where people were working at computers. Paul walked her to the manager's private suite to introduce her.

Yves Brouard was a wiry, energetic Frenchman, probably around forty. Paul let her know he was married and the father of two children.

After giving Paul a hug to welcome him home, Yves told him to get lost while he interviewed Hallie. He'd said it with a smile, yet she could tell Paul didn't like being dismissed that way. He pursed his lips before advising Hallie he'd come by for her in an hour.

"So—" Yves's eyes smiled at her in male admiration. "Paul tells me you need a job to stay in France for a while."

That was it? "Did he tell you why?"

He pulled on his earlobe. "No, but after meeting you I can understand the urgency to keep you here."

Oh, Paul, she moaned inwardly.

Without wasting time she told Yves she was a lay nun who'd been working as a sales clerk at Tati's in Paris. After receiving that information, his countenance changed.

"The twins and I became good friends. I don't know how long I'm going to be here doing service in the area, but I must find a job since I'm here on a working visa."

"Forgive me for making a false assumption," he muttered.

"If Paul didn't explain, then you couldn't have known. As he is Monsieur Rolland's son, this has put you in a difficult position, so please be honest if you can't use temporary help. I'll find something else."

He reached in his shirt pocket for a pack of cigarettes, then hesitated. "Will it bother you?"

"No."

After another moment's pause he changed his mind. "What experience have you had besides sales at a department store?"

"I received a secondary teaching degree from UCLA in Spanish with a French minor."

"Spanish you say?" His interest seemed to pick up.

"Yes. After graduation I became a stewardess for Trans-Chilean Airlines and worked for them until my husband died."

He frowned. "I'm sorry about your loss."

"So am I. After time passed, my focus changed and I became a lay nun. To earn my keep, I worked as a waitress in a Spanish-speaking restaurant in San Diego until I came to France."

"You must be fluent."

"Yes. My husband was Chilean. That helped."

"What about your skills on the computer?"

Something she'd told him had obviously caught his attention.

"I've used one since junior high."

"How long did you say you were planning to stay?"

"We're not sure."

Both of them looked up to see Vincent's hard-muscled frame in the doorway. She had no idea he'd been anywhere around the winery. How long had he been standing there? Her heart pounded so hard she felt sick with excitement.

Yves got to his feet. "I think we've found the right person to help Michel handle the new South American accounts."

"Go on."

As Yves related everything she'd told him, Vincent's eyes played over her with a burning intensity she'd never felt before.

"Michel's been doing double duty juggling them and his normal workload," Yves explained. "With Hallie's knowledge of Spanish, she could take over as soon as she's trained."

Vincent nodded. "Is Michel here?"

"It's his day off. I'd be happy to get her st—"

"I appreciate that, Yves, but you're still dealing with the new accounts I brought back from England. While you fax her mother superior in Paris and tell her Ms. Linn is on the payroll, I'll take her to my office and show her what's involved."

A tremor shook her body. Being alone with him was exactly what she'd hoped to avoid.

His dark eyes slid to hers once more. "If you don't feel it's something you'd be interested in doing, I have another idea," he murmured.

What could she say in front of his employee? "I'm very grateful for any job."

With unsteady fingers she opened her purse and looked up the fax number in the small notebook she carried. After she'd written the information down, she thanked Yves and got up to follow Vincent.

This time she made certain she didn't walk close enough for him to clasp her arm. She couldn't handle that right now or her trembling would give her away.

His office was situated on the ground floor of the chateau. The entrance lay directly opposite the winery office, an arrangement that made perfect sense.

According to the twins, merchants from all over the world came here to do business with him. He had staff who took new clients and tourists on tours of the wine cellars and the plant itself located east of the chateau.

Vincent ran a unique and lucrative family empire dating back close to four hundred years. It was self evident he had extraordinary business acumen, yet as far as Hallie was concerned his greatest success proved to be his remarkable children.

"Come inside." He'd unlocked the door for her.

His office place reflected a combination of a spacious seventeenth century drawing room meshed with the necessities of modern day technology.

On one wall hung an enormous tapestry showing a bird's eye view of the Rolland chateau and estate. On the opposite wall was an equally large map entitled A History of the Rolland Vineyards.

The vineyards were labeled to show the hectares, the yield, the type of grape, the time of maturity, the coveted awards for the best harvest of a certain year.

This was Vincent's inner sanctum. It made her want to spend hours in here and learn more about him. She couldn't lie to herself any longer. There was no one she enjoyed being around more than him.

What was she going to do?

He stood behind her. She could feel his body warmth, smell the soap he'd used in the shower that morning. She didn't dare turn around.

"I know it's overwhelming at first."

It was overwhelming all right. Her feelings bordered on hysteria. This time he hadn't even touched her, yet she was seized by longings that had set her on fire.

"Papa?" At the sound of Monique's familiar voice coming from another doorway, Hallie jumped in place, condemned by more guilt feelings. They were intensifying by the second. "I was hoping I'd fi— Oh— Hallie— I thought Papa said you'd gone sightseeing with Paul."

Hallie turned slowly in Monique's direction, attempting to exude an attitude of calm. What a joke!

"Before I did anything else, I felt it best to see about my job."

"That must have made Paul's day," Monique drawled her sarcasm in up-to-date American lingo. No one knew her brother like Monique did. She smiled at her father. "Have you given Hallie a job yet? She can do anything you know."

"So I'm finding out." Vincent's deep voice sounded strange. Husky. "If you came to give me a hug, I'm waiting."

"I do believe you've missed me," she said before flinging herself into her father's arms. Hallie envied Monique that privilege. "But I missed you much more, Papa. I'm so happy to be home."

"Amen to that, *petite.*"

She tossed her head back. "Do I have your permission to talk to Vivienne about training to learn her job? You told me that after I returned from Paris, we'd discuss it. Suzette's begging me to try to find a summer job with her in St. Genes, but I want to work here on the estate.''

His intrigued glance settled on Hallie. "What do you think?''

Hallie didn't want him to ask her. Every time they talked, he drew her in a little more until she didn't know who she was or what she was doing.

"I'm biased when it comes to Monique. I knew she was outstanding the minute I met her. Graduating top in her class came as no surprise to me.''

Vincent eyed his daughter with so much love, Hallie felt her throat swell. "I'm very proud of you.''

"You're lucky to have a daughter who's excited about working,'' Hallie added. "Too many young people I've met in my service are school dropouts, strung out on drugs, incapable of holding a job until they're rehabilitated.''

His gaze held hers briefly before he kissed Monique on the forehead and let go of her. "So you want to help with the tourists.''

"Yes!'' she cried excitedly.

"All right. You can go over to her office and tell her I gave you permission to start training.''

When Monique smiled like that, she was truly beautiful. Did the reminder of his wife still haunt Vincent in some secret place in his heart?

It was a question Hallie shouldn't be asking or even entertaining because it meant she was…jealous.

"*Merci*, Papa. Merci, Hallie. Oh—before I forget. Today is Etvige's birthday. I'm planning a little party for her. We won't do anything until she has served dinner.

"When she goes back in the kitchen to bring out the dessert, we'll turn off the lights and have a marzipan cake waiting for her. Can I borrow the car to pick it up from town?"

"Of course. Check with Paul. He's around here somewhere with my keys."

"I'll find him. I've already alerted Gaston and the others so they'll join us. Everyone's bringing a gift. I'm going to give her that dress I brought her from Paris."

The famous red dress.

Hallie imagined Vincent wouldn't be able to put the memory of that traumatic evening out of his mind for a long time. But when she peered at him through shuttered eyelids, he was ruffling his daughter's hair.

"Etvige will love it, *petite*. I was going to slip a bonus in her paycheck. Instead I'll give it to her tonight with a card. Will you buy one for me?"

"Of course, Papa. See you both later."

"Shut the door behind you," he called after her.

When they were alone again, he turned to Hallie. She thought he was going to launch into an explanation of her new job. Instead she felt a change in him.

"How long were you married to your Chilean husband?" His features had taken on a chiseled cast.

It stunned her that he wanted to talk about Raul.

"I—If you don't think my Spanish is good enough, that's all right. I'll find another job."

"That's not why I'm asking the question."

She raised startled eyes to his. "I don't understand."

"Paul has no idea the kind of pain you're still in."

Seconds passed before it registered that he thought she was still actively grieving for her husband.

"I'd rather not discuss my personal life."

"I wouldn't have brought up the past if I weren't worried about the extra burden you've taken on to come here and help Paul." His low toned utterance revealed grave concern.

"It's not a burden," she whispered. "Raul's gone on to a better place. We can thank God that Paul is still alive. I'm prepared to do whatever it takes to get him through this crisis so he'll be able to live a long, happy life." *Even if it's killing me to be near you.*

"Hallie— If I haven't said anything until now, I want you to know how grateful I am to you for watching over my children in Paris. When I see the way they turn to you, how they crave your approbation and preen under your praise, I realize you've filled a great void in their lives."

She shook her head. "You don't need to thank me. Your children are so easy to love. I think you and your twins are the luckiest people in the world to have each other."

He was standing too close. Another inch and he'd be touching her. "What about your family, Hallie? I've never heard you talk about them."

Her eyelids closed too late to prevent tears from beading her lashes.

"T-they're all gone."

Silence filled the room.

"What do you mean *gone?*"

Hallie couldn't talk about it. She turned around, pretending interest in the tapestry while she attempted to gather her composure.

"Tell me," he urged. Like warm honey spilling on her skin, she felt his hands slide to her shoulders from behind. He squeezed them gently. "I want to hear."

If he hadn't done that, she would have been all right. But once she felt the throb of his flesh through her blouse, it seemed to press on a hidden spring. A stream of long-suppressed emotions burst forth.

A sob escaped.

"Hallie—" he half groaned her name. "Let it out."

Helpless to combat his passionate entreaty she said, "They all died in the crash."

"Who's they?" he persisted.

"B-both sets of my grandparents, my parents, my husband's parents, his married brother and wife, my brother and his wife, my baby nephew and Raul."

"Holy mother of God."

He wrapped his arms fully around her and pulled her back against his chest. She'd borne her agony in silence for so long, to be able to share it with him for one fleeting moment was a luxury she welcomed.

"The jet went down in the Andes. Raul and I had just been married the day before. My parents had given us a big reception at our home in Bel Air. We were flying to Santiago for another reception when the plane lost power.

"There were 250 people aboard. Only six survived. Because of the inaccessible mountain terrain, we weren't found for a week.

"I was sure I was dead and had gone to some strange place. I couldn't see anything. All I could hear was this woman's voice who held my hand and told me not to give up. She kept my eyes covered. I heard her promise that help was on the way.

"Sometimes she sang to me. Sometimes she prayed and helped me to pray. She gave me hope when there was no hope.

"Then one day I heard other voices talking about a

plane crash. Someone told me I was being rescued. The next time I was aware of anything, I had awakened in a hospital.

"My eyes were bandaged and I couldn't move one of my legs. The doctor attending me told me I had snow blindness and a broken leg, but I would recover.

"I remember thinking it didn't matter about me. Where was the woman who'd watched over me? The person who'd prevented me from slipping away? Who was helping her?

"He said he would find out her name. There'd been one survivor who'd only needed a few days hospitalization before she'd been released.

"The next morning I felt a familiar hand cover mine. It was her voice that spoke to me. She said, "I heard you were asking for me, *señora*. I'm Sister Carlotta.""

While Hallie had been reliving the tragedy, she was aware that something else was happening. Vincent had started kissing her hair and temple.

He might think he was comforting her, but he'd aroused other feelings she couldn't ignore. Like coming out of a dream state, she was suddenly aware of the heat of their bodies from the back of her head to her legs.

Terrified of certain yearnings he'd evoked, she slipped out of his arms and sat down in the nearest chair. Without looking at him she said, "I'm sorry to have lost control like that."

His sudden intake of breath sounded like a whip cracking. "*Mon Dieu,* Hallie. It's a miracle you even function."

"There's a purpose in everything. I believe that, and have come to terms with it." She moistened her dry lips. "Yves mentioned new accounts in South America. Does this mean in several countries?"

Before he could answer, the twins came in through the outside door, Paul in the lead. Hallie shivered. If they'd happened on her and Vincent two minutes sooner…

"What's the deal, Papa? Monique said you were letting her take the car, but Hallie and I already have plans to go to St. Emilion." He'd started right off without any kind of greeting to his father.

His uncharacteristic rudeness reminded Hallie of the rebellious teens she'd worked with both in California and Paris.

By now Vincent was seated behind his desk. "Can't the three of you go together? Monique could use help planning Etvige's birthday fete for this evening."

Paul's surprised gaze flitted to his sister. "Are you sure it's today?"

"Positive!"

"While you're there, have lunch on me at the Trois Maroons. Hallie of all people will enjoy those cakes baked fresh from the Ursuline Sisters' 300 year old recipe."

He pulled some cash out of his wallet and held it up. Monique rushed around the side of his desk to kiss him.

"*Merci*, Papa!"

Hallie was the first out the door. No matter how she tried to rationalize it, her breakdown in Vincent's arms had put them on a more intimate footing. How could the twins not sense it?

Vincent's arrival in her life had blurred the lines separating the spiritual from the physical and emotional spheres of her existence. If things didn't change soon, she would be the one seeking Dr. Cluny's counsel.

CHAPTER SEVEN

"I HAVE a present for you, too, Etvige."

"Ah?" The housekeeper looked shocked.

Vincent had also thought the gift giving was over, but such wasn't the case.

Hallie handed Etvige a small, festively wrapped package from her brown skirt pocket. It was the same skirt she'd been wearing when he'd walked into his apartment and had seen the ring glittering on her finger.

That moment seemed to belong to a different time in a distant land.

Etvige undid the paper. She lifted the ribbon holding a red and white cloisonné enamel piece made in the shape of a heart. Love The Giver was written in the center.

The older woman turned to Hallie. "What a lovely gift."

"Whenever I was with the twins, they talked about you and Gaston with such affection, I thought you ought to know what kind of an impact you've had on them over the years."

"It's true," Monique murmured. Paul didn't say anything, but he managed to smile at them. It was a first for him since he'd been home.

Vincent drained the rest of his wine in order to prevent himself from walking around the table and pulling Hallie into his arms as he'd done earlier in the day.

He doubted any gesture could have meant more to

the childless couple who'd been with him and Pere for over ten years.

Etvige got up from the table. "Thank you, everyone." She sounded on the verge of tears. "Come along, Gaston."

He gathered up the rest of the gifts. Before leaving the table he patted Hallie's hand. Minou and her husband took that as their cue and excused themselves, too.

Finally it was just the family. Hallie fit right in. The haunting thought of her leaving one day in the future to enter a convent was anathema to Vincent.

He needed to hear more about this calling of hers. Obviously there was much more to it than he'd previously surmised.

That's what was torturing him now. It didn't help that she'd pulled away from him in his office before she'd finished telling him everything. He'd been left floundering in a new kind of hell.

But he had to acknowledge that whatever had caused her to tear herself away from his arms so abruptly was providential. If Paul had walked in on them while Vincent was covering her hair and temple with kisses, no explanation for his behavior would have satisfied his son.

On the other hand, he wouldn't be able to go to bed tonight until he'd heard all of her story. But how to get her alone without alerting his children?

Already Pere had set up his chess game while Monique and Hallie cleared the remains of the birthday festivities.

Judging by the way Paul's fingers tapped on the edge of the table as if he were playing the bongos, he wanted to bolt and take Hallie with him. Instead he had the choice of spending the evening watching her and Pere

enjoy themselves. Or he could take himself off somewhere and worry everyone sick.

Vincent couldn't tolerate either possibility.

He ached for his son whose infatuation over Hallie
had led him down a hopeless, treacherous emotional
path. Maybe—

"Paul? How's the cottage coming for Hallie?"

His son stopped his fiddling for a minute. "Bernard's
got all the plumbing to work. He had to replace the lock.
A cleaning crew is coming tomorrow, then it'll be ready
to furnish."

"Why wait till tomorrow?"

Paul shot his father a puzzled glance. "What do you
mean?"

"If we put some muscle into it, you and I could do
a lot better job. What do you say we get to work?
Monique can help us. Who knows? By the time Pere
declares 'check mate,' Hallie might be able to settle in
her own apartment tonight."

A light flared in his son's eyes. "Let's do it!" He
pushed himself away from the table.

It was another small victory to draw closer to his son,
even if Hallie represented the sole incentive behind
Paul's capitulation.

"I'll change my clothes and meet you in the utility
room in five minutes."

"I've got to change, too."

They left the dining room together. On the way out,
Pere exchanged glances with Vincent. His grandfather
gave him a barely discernible nod of approval for the
truce achieved, no matter how short-lived it might be.

If Pere had any idea there was a lot more on
Vincent's mind than Paul's happiness, he probably
wouldn't live through the experience.

Vincent was supposed to have gained some wisdom over the last eighteen years. So how come he was busy plotting and devising means to find himself alone with the woman his son had been fantasizing about for the last nine months?

Maybe Vincent was losing his mind...

"Eh voilà! Your cottage is ready."

After another educational session with Pere on the fine points of chess, Monique had dragged Hallie out the back of the chateau to the cottage being prepared for her.

Cottage was the wrong word. The apartment was totally charming with a tiny seventeenth century print in burgundy and yellow on the walls. There was a salon, a small dining room, kitchen, bathroom and bedroom furnished with two twin beds and a fabulous armoire. There was even a phone.

Period pieces of furniture and paintings had been placed throughout the suite with a flair that bespoke Monique's artistic hand.

"Do you like it?"

"You already know the answer to that." Hallie hugged her hard. "Thank you, Monique. I'm going to feel like a princess while I'm here."

"Papa and Paul helped get it ready."

"I wondered where they'd disappeared to."

"Would you like me to sleep with you tonight so you won't feel lonely away from the chateau?"

Much as Hallie adored Monique, she would have preferred to be alone so she could phone Gaby. Hallie had only called her friend twice since leaving San Diego. Once on Gaby's birthday and the other time at Christmas.

Hallie had planned to phone her one more time after she returned to California. But she'd been knocked off her axis by a situation she couldn't allow to go on much longer.

Gaby was the voice of reason. If necessary, she and Max would be brutally frank with Hallie. Yet how could she turn down Monique's offer?

After what Paul had done, his sister needed a sounding board. Unfortunately that person couldn't be Suzette or any of her girlfriends. Besides Hallie, only her father and Pere could be trusted in a matter as serious as this.

"I'd love it. Let's get our things."

On their way out of the cottage, they ran into the men who were talking to Bernard.

Once introductions were made he handed Hallie her key. "I have a duplicate in case you lose it."

She thanked him, then hurried into the chateau with Monique. A lay nun's wardrobe only filled one suitcase. It didn't take long for Hallie to pack. On the way out, she tucked a novel under her arm from Monique's well stocked bookshelf.

The French girl grabbed what she would need for the night and they returned to the cottage straight away.

"What are you doing?" Paul demanded the second he saw his sister with an overnight bag.

He and his father were waiting for them in the salon. Hallie tried to avoid feasting her eyes on Vincent. She'd done enough of that at dinner. But it was virtually impossible not to stare when he looked so incredibly male and sexy in a pair of well-worn jeans and black T-shirt.

Those weren't the thoughts a lay nun should be having. How did she shut them out?

"I asked Monique to stay with me. As long as you're all here, let me thank you for getting it ready for me so fast. The apartment is absolutely beautiful. I thought we'd christen my new home away from home by taking turns reading Colette's *Seven Dialogues of Beasts*."

"We are?"

She turned to Monique. "Maybe I'm mistaken, but didn't you once tell me I *had* to read it?"

"My daughter's right," Vincent interjected. "It's a very funny story told from a cat and dog's point of view."

Not wanting to leave Paul out, Hallie said, "Why don't you stay and read with us before we go to bed, Paul? I need a lot of help with my French. Probably as much as you needed with English last fall," she added when he looked like he was ready to say no.

He made a strange face. "I'll read for a little while."

Vincent smiled. "I think it sounds like fun. Mind if I join you?"

Hallie couldn't believe her plan to avoid thinking about Vincent for one night had backfired so completely.

"The more the merrier," she quipped.

The next hour turned out to be one of the most memorable and delightful nights of Hallie's life. Everyone got into the parts. When it came time for Hallie to read, she gave it her best shot.

To their credit, the Rolland family managed to contain their amusement. At first. But when she tried to pronounce the low gnarling sound the dog made in French, it came out with a Spanish accent.

Vincent burst into deep rich laughter. It resounded throughout the room. Soon the twins had joined their father.

She caught him wiping his eyes. In that split second when their gazes collided, Hallie knew she was in love for the second time in her life. Passionately, wildly in love with this man.

A blush filled her cheeks.

She closed the book. "I think I've entertained all of you long enough." With effort, she looked away from him.

"All good things have to come to an end, unfortunately." Her host got to his feet. "Come on, Paul. Tomorrow will be here before we know it. Hallie? Michel Viret should be in the winery office by eight in the morning. When you're ready, he'll train you."

"Thank you for everything," her voice trembled. "Good night."

Paul lingered at the door. "You're not going to be playing chess with Pere tomorrow night are you?"

His loaded question brought the first discordant note into an unforgettable evening.

"No. Actually I'm going to meet Father Olivier at the church."

She could have predicted Paul's mutinous reaction. Vincent's was another matter.

Though he stood behind his son, he was taller and she could see him well enough. His jaw had hardened. All traces of the happy, carefree man of the last hour had vanished. Why the sudden change in him?

"Then I'll drive you." Paul's declaration bordered on an ultimatum. Hallie recognized this wasn't the time to frustrate his plans.

"I'd appreciate that."

Their father said, "I'm afraid I have an engagement tomorrow evening and will need the car."

Was Vincent going to see a woman?

Hallie couldn't bear the thought of it. Monique didn't act the least bit happy about it either.

Vincent eyed the twins. "I guess we're going to have to go to town in the morning and buy each of you a car."

It was hard for Hallie not to laugh at the surprised look on their faces.

"But I thought—"

"We all need transportation, Paul," Vincent broke in quietly. "At one time I'd assumed you two could share a car, but I can see that's not going to work.

"You both fulfilled your part of the bargain by getting top grades at school and making your father proud. Just remember one thing. There aren't any Ferrari or Maserati dealerships in St. Genes. You'll have to pick out something French."

Hallie chuckled. Vincent picked up on it and smiled at her across the expanse. Whatever had been bothering him a few moments ago seemed to have passed.

Everyone knew how much Paul loved Italian cars, but for once he didn't protest. If anything he looked totally taken back by his father's generosity. In view of the fact that he'd spent the money earmarked for a car on that horribly expensive ring, naturally he would be.

"Merci, Papa."

For Paul to call his father papa again meant Vincent was making strides. *Good, good, good,* Hallie repeated under her breath.

Monique flew to her father and hugged him.

Turning away from the happy scene, Hallie disappeared into the bathroom to get ready for bed. The phone call to Gaby would have to wait until tomorrow.

A little while later when lights were out and they'd climbed under their covers, Hallie heard Monique say her name. She turned back on her pillow.

"What is it?"

"If you decide to take your vows, could you do it here? There's a convent run by the Dominicans near Pomerol where Papa owns a vineyard."

Monique, Monique.

Hallie grasped the sheet, drawing it to her chin. "I could, but my goal is to teach young people in South America. There are poverty stricken areas where the government doesn't pay for education."

The French girl groaned. "South America— Why would you go there? It's so far away."

The time had come to tell Monique the things Hallie had confided to Vincent. For some reason she didn't dread relating her history now.

"If my husband Raul hadn't died in the plane crash, we would have made our home in Chile where he was born and raised."

She could hear Monique's mind working. "I knew he had a Hispanic name, but I didn't realize you'd married a Chilean."

"I'd just graduated from college and wanted adventure. We met while I was an airline attendant. He worked for an American based oil company and made a lot of flights from Santiago to Los Angeles.

"We dated for a year, fell in love and got married." In the next few minutes Monique was in full possession of the facts.

"Both your families? Everybody dead?" The horror in Monique's voice spoke volumes.

"Yes. But Sister Carlotta was there holding my hand. We talked every day until I was released from the hospital into her care. The nuns in Santiago took me in. They were wonderful."

"Just like you," Monique whispered.

"Thank you," Hallie whispered back. "When I told

Sister Carlotta I'd like to become one of them and teach in the poor regions she'd been talking about, she said I wouldn't be ready until I'd let go of my grief. And before I did that, I needed to get back in touch with my roots.

"At her urging, I returned to California. She said if I needed help, I could call on the holy mother at the Dominican convent in San Diego.

"So I flew to Los Angeles, but I couldn't handle all the memories. As soon as I sold my parents' home, I sent the proceeds to Sister Carlotta's convent as a gift. After that I went straight to the convent in San Diego, ready to join the sisters so I could return to South America.

"But the holy mother said I should take more time to consider my decision because it wasn't an easy life. She impressed on me I needed to be absolutely certain a life devoted to God was the right thing to do for me.

"Would I like to work in the order's outreach program and do service in the community? When I said yes, she arranged for me to wait on tables at a restaurant run by a Mexican family in San Diego. In time I met my dear friend Gaby and we decided to room together.

"After that everything started to improve. I could tell I was healing and I enjoyed helping people. Then my friend moved out of our apartment and got married.

"I visited with the holy mother again hoping to take my vows, but she said I still hadn't given myself a long enough time to understand all I'd be giving up. I was so upset, I argued with her.

"That in itself proved the discipline of a nun hadn't yet taken hold of me. I felt like a fool, but she was patient with me and suggested I try the outreach program in Paris.

"Just one more year," she said, "then we'll see how you feel then."

Little did Hallie know that her real test would come in the form of the Rolland family.

"I'm so glad Paul and I went into Tati's that day and met you!"

Hallie's eyes prickled with tears. "So am I," she confessed.

"I just wish you could stay here permanently, but I know you're not in love with my brother."

"What does one have to do with the other?"

"Papa told me you're only here to let Paul down gently."

"I see." Because it was true, Hallie decided not to qualify Vincent's explanation.

"Hallie? What if you met a man you could love again... Do you think you'd still want to be a nun?"

Vincent's image swam before her eyes.

"That's a good question, Monique. I can't answer it. To marry again would satisfy the selfish part of me. But as a nun, I could do more good in the world."

"Pere Maurice says a good marriage requires unselfishness on both sides to make it work. He also says a man and a woman are doing God's work when they raise a good family."

Monique was priceless. So was Pere. "He's right on both counts. However my concern at the moment is Paul and his mental state."

"I know. I wish I could get him to take out Suzette. She's always had a crush on him."

"There's only one problem with a crush," Hallie said. "It's all about the person who has the crush. The other person's emotions aren't involved."

"You're talking about Paul aren't you."

"And Luc," Hallie was quick to point out. "He couldn't stop teasing you last night."

"Luc's nice, but—"

"But he doesn't take your breath away? Don't worry. One day someone's going to come along who'll knock your socks off."

"I thought you said that was a dated expression."

Hallie grinned. "It is, but I happen to like it."

"I think Papa's been seeing a woman while we've been away." Monique made the leap to her father so fast, Hallie's heart turned over.

"Why do you say that?"

"He's acting different. I don't mean just about Paul. Lately he seems like—I don't know—like he's excited about something. Lucie, the girl who roomed with me, said Papa was so gorgeous she was surprised he hadn't gotten married years ago. Maybe now that Paul and I are older, that's what he's planning."

"Why don't you just come out and ask him if he's involved with someone special?"

"I'm afraid to."

"Monique—if he's met a woman important to him, then you can be sure she's a wonderful person."

"As long as she can make him happy," came the subdued aside.

"After being single this long, he wouldn't choose anyone you and Paul couldn't learn to love, too. Trust me. Over the last week I've discovered that you twins truly are your father's whole world. Look how much fun he had tonight."

"I know. I wanted it to last forever."

So did I.

"Night, Monique."

"Good night, Hallie."

* * *

"How's it going? Is Michel working you too hard?"

"Not at all," Hallie said, but Vincent's voice caused her to lose her concentration. A line of gibberish flashed on the computer monitor. She deleted it, but not fast enough to see the curve of his sensuous mouth out of the corner of her eye.

Michel was seated next to her. He turned in Vincent's direction. "She's already making my life easier. I was about to show her around the shipping room."

"I'll take her."

Hallie's pulse raced at his proprietorial tone.

"It would be no problem, Vincent."

"Lunch is ready at the chateau."

"Ah." The other man nodded as if in resignation. "Of course." He spread his hands in that typical French way with palms open and glanced at her. "Then I'll see you back here at three."

"Hallie won't be back until tomorrow. She's still getting settled in."

Hallie's purse lay in the bottom drawer of the desk. She reached for it, trying to hide her dismay over Vincent's cool tone. It bordered on rudeness. She'd never seen him treat anyone like that before.

"Thank you for being such a patient teacher, Michel." She stood up. "I'll be here at eight in the morning."

"It was my pleasure."

She followed her host's long strides out of the winery office. He walked over to his car parked in front of his office and waited for her to catch up to him. Hallie didn't understand when he opened the passenger door and helped her inside.

After he got in behind the wheel of the car, she

flashed him a puzzled glance. "I thought lunch was ready."

"Minou always has food ready and waiting if you're hungry." A tiny nerve pulsed at his temple. "Michel is the office lothario. I wanted him to know you're off limits. He doesn't care if you're a lay nun."

"I appreciate your concern, Vincent, but I can take care of myself."

"Not from my vantage point. While you were working, the man was eating you alive with his eyes."

Hallie had felt the other man come on a little too strong, but she hadn't expected Vincent to pick up on it.

"As soon as you're trained, you can use the computer in my office. I conduct the bulk of my business over the phone."

More than ever Hallie needed to talk to Gaby.

"I thought we'd take advantage of the time to buy groceries for your kitchen. You're welcome to eat at the chateau anytime, but you'll need food when you want to relax at the cottage.

"There's an excellent fromagerie in Pully, another little town five miles from here. At lunchtime they sell ham and cheese croissants that melt in your mouth."

Vincent had no idea what he was doing to her. What if Paul found out?

"Where are the twins?"

"I would imagine they're taking their friends for a ride in their new cars."

He started up the engine and they drove off. When they reached the gate to the estate, he turned in the other direction. The June air was so warm she opened the window.

"I remember my first car. It was the most thrilling day of my life."

"I wouldn't know," he muttered. "I had to make do with a bike till after I was married. Even then, it was Pere's car. We shared."

Everything she told him made her love him that much more. "So how old were you when you finally got one of your own?"

"I was twenty-seven and had been out of college two years."

"No Ferrari?"

His lips twitched. "Hardly. I had to be able to fit in two children and Pere."

Vincent—

They reached the quaint, medieval town in no time. In between visits to the marché and patisserie, Vincent fed her croissants and fresh, juicy plums. She felt like they were a divinely happy married couple out shopping for the day. They talked about anything and everything.

It was one of those moments she wanted to freeze for all time.

Three hours later they returned to the cottage. He helped her inside with the groceries and started shelving them.

This was bad.

She hadn't put up any kind of fight to shut him out today. Now that it was time for him to go, she wanted desperately for him to stay. Her heart pounded so hard, she felt feverish.

"Why do you want to return to South America?"

He'd posed the question just as she'd put the yogurts in the fridge and had shut the door.

Monique hadn't lost any time telling him about last

night's conversation. His daughter was frightened of changes in her life she could see coming.

When Hallie turned around, he was standing right in front of her, preventing her from moving without brushing up against him. His eyes trapped hers with fiery intensity.

"Do you know in your heart it's a call from God? Or do you feel it's the only way to pay Sister Carlotta back for helping you hang on until you were rescued?"

Hallie had been asking herself those questions for the last week. She finally shook her head. "I don't know," she murmured. Then, "I don't know!" Her cry of anguish hovered in the air.

"Monique's terrified that when Paul wakes up from this dream he's in and lets you go, you'll leave."

She lowered her eyes. "I'm aware of that."

"Couldn't you remain a lay nun here in St. Genes if you wanted to? Wouldn't it still accomplish the same thing? You'd be serving God and honoring Sister Carlotta."

She took a shuddering breath. "It isn't that simple, Vincent."

I couldn't bear to be around you for the rest of my life and not be your wife.

"Why not?" he demanded. His breathing had grown shallow. "My daughter needs you in a way Paul never did. She's going to require some reassurance soon, or another one of my children will end up in the hospital."

"Vincent—don't you know that's because she's worried about you?" Hallie blurted.

His black brows furrowed. "You're talking in riddles."

"I'm not trying to." She bit her lip. Maybe she was telling tales out of school, but he needed to understand

everything that was going on with his children if he
hoped to help them.

"Monique says you're different since you brought
them home from Paris. She thinks you've fallen in love
with someone, and that you're waiting for the right time
to tell them you're getting married."

CHAPTER EIGHT

VINCENT ached to crush Hallie in his arms, but if he did that, it would go against every principle he believed in.

Somehow he found the strength to back away from her.

She might not be wearing a habit, but she was a lay nun. Yesterday he'd held her in his arms to give her comfort. Today he had no such excuse.

"Is it true?" Her beautiful eyes, so clear and fathomless, beseeched him to tell her.

He had no doubts she was asking for Monique's sake. Once again that female intuition of his daughter's was dead on. Long ago he'd learned never to underestimate her.

But heaven forgive him, he wanted to believe Hallie was also asking for her own sake. How was it possible to be this on fire for her and not have those feelings and desires reciprocated?

No matter the love she felt for her deceased husband, the two of them had only been married twenty-four hours.

Vincent had already spent a week with her. He knew in his gut she wasn't indifferent to him.

"Yes," he admitted. "There is someone, but I haven't asked her to marry me yet."

"I see."

Not by a flicker of an eyelash or a movement in her throat did she betray what she was really thinking.

Vincent felt like he was standing on the edge of a precipice that was ready to give way.

"Before I do something that's going to change all our lives, I have to be certain Paul won't go off the deep end again. He might succeed next time."

A moan came out of her. "We can't let that happen. I'm doing everything in my power to stop this fantasy of his."

"Don't you think I know that?" he asked emotionally.

She nodded. "The trouble is, these things can't be rushed. What I'm hoping is that this evening whe—"

"Hallie?"

There was a knock on the door. It was Paul. Her gaze flew to Vincent's in alarm.

"Hallie? Papa? Are you in there?"

Vincent squeezed her arm. "I'll get it. You finish putting the groceries away."

After a few minutes Hallie heard footsteps crossing the hardwood floors. "Hello, Hallie."

She put a cereal box in the cupboard, then swung around. "You look happy with yourself. What do you think of your new car?"

He actually smiled. "It's great. It even has a sun roof."

"You lucky thing. Has everyone in St. Genes seen it already?"

"Just about." He chuckled. "Do you want to go for a ride?"

"I'd love to." She checked her watch. It was ten after four. "Can we go at six? You can show me all its amazing features until seven when I have to be at the church."

His smile faded. Once again she'd put him off, but it was the only way to handle him. "Sure."

"The thing is, your father helped me get a week's worth of groceries. Now I'd like to fix dinner. After that I have to shower and make an important call."

She walked over to one of the drawers and pulled out a marzipan bar. "Here." She put it in his hand. "This is my contribution. Put it in your glove compartment for a rainy day."

"What does that mean?"

Hallie smoothed the hair off her forehead. "Haven't I taught you that? Hmph. I guess not. A rainy day is a day when things aren't going that great."

After digesting her explanation he proceeded to open the wrapper and take a big bite.

"Paul—didn't you understand what I said?"

"Yes." He kept on eating until it was gone, then tossed the wrapper in the waste basket.

"I guess you didn't stop for lunch."

"Luc and I ate a big one."

She frowned. "What's wrong?"

"I was having a great day until I came to get you, but you always have something else you've got to do, or someplace you've just come from, or somewhere you have to go. It seems like things are a lot different since Paris."

He was starting to crack.

"They are. The three of us only had certain days and times of the week when we could be together. If you'd been with me around the clock, like Beauregard is with Pere, you would have realized what my schedule was like."

He stared hard at her. "You never stop."

"I can't. I'm afraid it's the way I'm made."

Paul had a habit of tapping on things. Right now it was the kitchen counter. Suddenly he stopped.

"I'll be back at six."

"Thanks, Paul."

She walked him to the door. "See you soon— à bientôt!"

After she'd locked it, she ran through the apartment to the bedroom. It was a little after eight in the morning in San Diego. If Gaby's toddler was still asleep, Hallie hated to wake her up, but this was an emergency.

Be home, Gaby. Please be home and please answer.

The voice mail came on. She was about to hang up and try again after her shower when someone picked up.

"Hello?"

"Gaby?"

After a slight hesitation, "Hallie! It's so wonderful to hear your voice you can't imagine. Are you back in California?"

At this point Hallie was so emotional, she lost control. Like a waterfall the tears spilled down her face. She couldn't stop them.

"No. I'm still in France," she said between sobs. "Gaby—I'm in trouble."

The next time Hallie checked her watch it was quarter to six. She couldn't believe they'd been talking an hour and a half.

"I have to run. Paul's going to be here for me in a few minutes."

"Wait—before we hang up, tell me one thing. You don't honestly believe there's another woman—"

Hallie used the end of the sheet to wipe her eyes. "Vincent's a normal, red blooded male. Of course there are other women."

"Hallie—"

"If you're talking about *the* woman, I don't know. He has plans to go somewhere tonight. All I can say is, if she does exist, then she must be awfully understanding for him to never bring her around. But the situation with Paul is precarious. He doesn't dare make a wrong move."

"I think he gave himself away when he asked you to remain in St. Genes as a lay nun for his daughter's sake. It sounds like a smoke screen to me."

"I—I want to believe that, too," Hallie's voice trembled. "But what if I'm wrong?"

"Do you remember when I ran away from Max?"

Hallie sniffed. "How could I forget? I'm the one who told you to fly home to New Jersey."

"And have you forgotten we resolved everything? I'm married to the man of my dreams. Are you listening, Hallie?"

"Yes."

"Here's the bottom line. Both the holy mothers said you weren't ready to take binding vows. Now you can see why. You were sent to France for a reason. You have to stay there and let this whole thing unravel itself until the answers are clear."

"I don't have any choice as long as Paul's so fragile."

"You know what I think? You're the most wonderful woman I've ever known. I love you, Hallie. You're not going to be in torment forever."

"Promise?"

"I do. Call me anytime. I mean it!"

"I will. Thanks, Gaby."

Hallie hung up and dashed into the shower. Though

their conversation hadn't resolved anything, she felt better for having been able to unload to her trusted friend.

However by the time she'd put on a clean blouse and skirt, one thing had become clear to her.

Since coming to St. Genes, Hallie loved being totally involved with every member of the Rolland family. It was because she'd been raised in a loving, dynamic family herself, and missed all that interaction.

The thought of becoming part of a community of devout sisters for the rest of her life didn't hold the same appeal anymore. Naturally she would love the teaching part, but the lack of connection to any one person would always be missing.

Her thoughts darted back to last week. When she'd known the time was drawing near to say a permanent goodbye to Paul and Monique in Paris, she'd sensed she was going to suffer another great loss. It put serious doubts in her mind about her suitability for the professed life.

To add to her conflicted state, she'd met Vincent. His mere existence had the power to awaken the sensual side of her nature she'd thought had been dead and buried with Raul.

Tonight she had to face the truth about something else she'd been fighting.

She *was* a more worldly lay nun, otherwise she would have phoned Mother Marie-Claire for help instead of Gaby. Yet were her friend's words any less inspired?

Both the holy mothers said you weren't ready to take binding vows. Now you can see why. You were sent to France for a reason. You have to stay there and let this whole thing unravel itself until the answers are clear.

Three hours later, one of Hallie's suspicions about herself was verified beyond question.

After Father Olivier's introduction, the teen youth group at the church exhibited great enthusiasm over the idea of the new American giving English lessons. It was decided classes would be held at the church from seven to eight-thirty on Monday and Wednesday nights throughout the summer.

Hallie was excited at the prospect of putting her teaching degree to real use. But it wasn't until she got in the car where Paul had been waiting to drive her home that she realized her true joy lay in going back to the chateau, to the people she'd grown to love. To the twins, Pere, Beauregard. *Vincent.*

No matter how things played out here, whatever the future held, she knew she would never feel complete if she became professed.

Being able to admit that to herself at long last caused a measure of calm to seep into her soul. Totally absorbed in her own thoughts, she was suddenly aware they weren't moving anymore.

She blinked.

Paul had driven her to the same heavenly spot on the river where Vincent had brought her that first morning.

It was like déjà vu in one way. The sun had barely dipped below the horizon. The glorious scene was as picture perfect as before. But the same man wasn't at the wheel. Furthermore, she smelled alcohol. Paul must have had a drink while he waited for her, but Hallie wondered how many.

There was no mistaking the odor that mingled with the smell of his new car. She knew because she'd already been on an hour's ride with Paul before he'd driven her to the church. She remembered remarking on how much she loved getting into a brand-new car just off the lot.

Now that she thought about it, she hadn't been able to talk him into attending the church group activity with her. She'd hoped he'd find some girls his own age to enjoy, but he'd muttered something about having another place to go and would come by for her later.

A lot of college kids drank. Before Paul's accident, he'd talked about attending college in Bordeaux in the fall where she presumed he would experiment like so many others.

But she had a feeling this was different, that he'd been drinking alone. A new car couldn't fix Paul's depression. It might even have exacerbated it because what he really wanted was unattainable. Vincent needed to know about this troubling development.

But he wasn't here to help her with his son, and Hallie was no psychiatrist.

What she said to Paul now might not be the right thing, yet she felt something was required of her to appease him before they went home.

"If this is your favorite place, I can see why."

He was lying against the seat with his arm extended across the back. In a slow movement he angled his head toward her. His eyes were veiled.

"It's my father's," came the blunt reply, "but you already know that."

She felt heat swirl to her face like a geyser.

"Louis, one of my father's employees, was working in the vineyard and saw the two of you together." Paul let out a sound that could have been anger or pain, probably both. "He told everybody at the plant that Papa has a girlfriend."

Her body quavered in place. *I'm so sorry Paul.*

"At least you don't deny being here with him. That's

the one thing about you I can always count on. Your rock gut honesty.''

His hand crept to the ends of her hair lying against her neck. ''I told everyone to forget what they were thinking, because you were a lay nun.

''That shut everybody up, but it couldn't stop what they were thinking. It hasn't stopped what I've been thinking.''

He tugged on some strands he'd wrapped around his fingers. Not hard, but with just enough pressure to make her realize how angry he was.

''You and Papa were making love when I came to the cottage this afternoon and interrupted you. I could tell it the second he opened the door.

''A different man than the one I've lived with for eighteen years stood there looking happy in that certain way I've seen Jules's father look after being in the bedroom with his wife for a few hours.

''Papa kept talking to me. I knew why. He was trying to give you time to get dressed. When I went in the kitchen, I hardly recognized you. You looked...*so alive*.

''Damn you, Hallie—'' The last came out sounding like a sob.

''You're wrong you know,'' she said softly. ''Only one of the Rolland men has ever kissed me. That was you, Paul.''

He bolted upright. His face held a strange twist of confusion and despair. She could tell he wanted to believe her, but the angry part of him was dominant.

''I want you to leave St. Genes—'' The veins stood out in his neck above the collar of his Polo shirt. ''Just get out of my sight, and never come back!''

He was hurting like a wounded bull. She'd seen other

teens in an inebriated condition, but this was Paul. He was his father's son.

Vincent had reached the apex of his pain when he'd walked in on her and Paul in Paris. There'd been no reasoning with him then. There'd be no reasoning with Paul now. Not until he'd slept this off.

What to do.

She glanced out the window. Though it was getting dark fast, she knew her way back to the chateau. Yet she didn't dare leave Paul by the river where he might get it into his head to jump in. Vincent had already warned her of the danger.

"Paul—I realize you'd like to be by yourself right now, but this area is still unfamiliar to me. I'm afraid I'll get lost if I try to find my way back home alone. How much have you had to drink? You shouldn't be driving if you've been drinking."

"I've only had a couple." He snapped and jerked his head toward her. "Do you swear before God my father didn't take you to bed?"

She swallowed hard. "You don't need me to answer that question because you know the truth."

A shudder rippled through his taut frame. "I know what I saw. If it didn't happen yet, it's going to!"

"Wrong again, Paul." She suddenly knew what she had to do.

"If you would be kind enough to drive me to the cottage, I'll pack my bag, then go to St. Genes. There'll be a train leaving for Paris tonight. I intend to be on it."

His head bobbed in reaction.

"It's too bad you've been drinking. Otherwise I'd ask you to drive me to Paris in your new car and leave me at Clairemont Abbey,'' she added to make sure he knew she was deadly serious.

That remark seemed to galvanize him into action. To her everlasting relief he started the car and backed around. He didn't say another word during the short trip back to the cottage.

When he pulled up in front she said, ''You can stay here and wait for me, or come in while I pack. Whatever you prefer.''

It took her five minutes to throw everything inside her suitcase. She grabbed her passport out of the dresser and slipped it in her purse. When she returned to the lounge, Paul was standing in the open doorway holding on to the frame.

He looked stunned to see she was ready to travel.

''You're kidding about leaving. You're trying to pay me back for being cruel to you.''

''Not at all. I didn't come to St. Genes to divide your family or create gossip that hurts you. You and Monique are home with your father again. My mission here is accomplished.

''If you don't want to drive me, I'll phone the chateau and ask your sister to take me to the station.''

Paul shook his head. ''Don't leave, Hallie. I didn't mean the things I said.''

''I know you didn't.'' Though her heart was breaking, she smiled at him. ''But it's time for me to go.''

She started for the entry, forcing him to move while she shut and locked the door.

There was no sign of Vincent's car. He was still out for the evening. A pain pierced her heart. Whether he was with another woman or not, it couldn't be her concern any longer.

With Paul lagging behind, she put the case in the

back seat herself, then climbed in the front and waited for him to start the car again.

His bloodshot eyes stared helplessly at her. "You can't just walk out! What about your new job? Your classes at the church?"

"I know I can depend on you to explain everything."

Paul watched as she put the key to the cottage in his glove compartment. He looked on the verge of tears. "If Monique knew about this, she'd find a way to stop you."

"That's why it's best that you drive me. By the time she wakes up tomorrow, I'll be in Paris and unavailable."

"Don't say that!" he cried.

"Paul—on the strength of the friendship we share, will you please take me to town now?"

Tears glazed his eyes. He wiped at them with his forearm, then started the car. His shoulders shook with silent sobs all the way to the train station.

This time he got out first and carried her bag while she hurried inside to buy a ticket.

"Un aller," she told the woman. *One way.*

They hadn't reached the station any too soon. The next train for Paris would be arriving any minute. It would be the last one until morning.

"The night is so beautiful, let's wait on the platform, shall we?"

Paul's face was a study in agony as he followed her out to the tracks. "If you cared about me at all, you wouldn't do this."

Hallie took a fortifying breath, trying to adapt to his mood swings. "I love you like I loved my own brother, John."

As she spoke, she could hear the train coming into the station.

Paul's body went stock-still. "I knew you had family, but you never mentioned you had a brother."

"He was my only sibling. Two years older than I. In many ways you're a lot like him. Or like he was… Not in looks, but in character."

"What happened to him?"

"Ask Monique. She'll tell you everything. The point is, that's probably why I felt such a connection to you when we first met."

The train came to a stop. It would only wait long enough for those with tickets to get on board. Then it would take off again. She hurried to the steps and climbed on. No one else seemed to be getting on. They were alone.

Hallie sensed his reluctance to hand her the suitcase.

"I love you like a brother, Paul." Tears began to well. "When you tried to take your own life, I thought I couldn't bear it if I lost another one.

"Please let your father help you. He loves you so much." Her voice caught on a sob. "So does Monique. So does Pere. Everyone needs family. With one like yours behind you, you'll have a beautiful life. *Au revoir, mon cher ami.*"

The train lurched, then started out of the station. She held on to the side rail and waved to him.

"Wait!" he suddenly cried out and started running alongside her car, but the train had gained momentum. He couldn't catch up.

She watched until he was a speck in the light from the station. Then the train rounded a curve and everything went dark.

* — * — *

After a long, drawn out evening at the Hotel Florissant in St. Genes, Vincent couldn't get back to the chateau fast enough.

Gossip abounded in the tightly knit region. Vincent wanted to offset any talk about his interest in Hallie, so he'd spent an evening dining and dancing with Madelaine Beguey. She was a striking brunette divorcée he'd been out with once before. Hopefully being with her would confound everyone who knew him.

By morning the winery would explode with the latest morsel of misinformation. That was his plan. He was prepared to do anything to prevent Paul from being hurt.

His headlights picked up the outline of the twins' cars parked in the front courtyard. It was after one. He assumed his children were asleep.

Normally he parked his car in front, too, but a compulsion stronger than his conscience prevailed. He drove around the back of the chateau, wondering if Hallie was still up.

His heart thudded in his chest to see that a light was still burning in the salon. After he pulled around to the front of his office, he sat there for ten minutes while a war waged inside him.

No matter what plausible pretext he used, if he were to go over and knock on her door, it would undo all his earlier machinations to throw those off the scent whose idle talk could injure his children.

His desire to see Hallie would have to wait until morning.

It was going to be a long, endless night.

Not daring to look in the direction of her cottage again, he got out of his car and entered his office. There was always work he could do. In fact now was the best time to make overseas calls to his sales people in countries with an eight to ten-hour time difference.

Throwing his suit jacket and tie over a chair, he undid his shirt part way and rolled up his sleeves. After sitting down at his desk, he reached for a basket of files and opened the top one.

But it only took him twenty seconds to realize he wasn't going to be able to concentrate on anything. Tomorrow he'd install Hallie in here with him and train her himself. If he couldn't be with her any other way, he could at least share his business with her.

People came and went from his office all day long. The door was always open. Soon everyone would learn she was the lay nun his children had befriended in Paris. In time the rumors would dissipate.

And then what?

He let out a groan, unable to answer that question.

"Papa?"

The tone of alarm in Monique's voice coming at this hour of the morning kicked off his adrenaline. He looked up in time to see his daughter's robed figure dart toward him. By the time he got to his feet she'd thrown herself into his arms, completely dissolved in tears.

"What's wrong, *petite?*"

"It's Paul."

This was the second time in a week a cold sweat broke out on his body.

"Where is he?"

"In his bedroom. He came to my room earlier tonight demanding to know what Hallie had told me about her family. I could smell alcohol. He'd been drinking heavily.

"I thought he knew about the tragedy. After I explained everything, he muttered something about doing the unforgivable and ran to his room. I followed him, but he locked the door on me and told me go away.

"He couldn't stop sobbing, Papa. I got so frightened I told him I was going to find you, but he swore me to secrecy. When I asked him why, he said that if you were to find out what he'd done, you would never forgive him."

She paused long enough to catch her breath. "I promised him I wouldn't say anything, but after what Dr. Maurois told me, I knew I had to tell you." Her small hands gripped his arms. "I thought you'd never get home. Then I saw your car from the window, but you never came up to bed, so I hurried down here."

Vincent hugged his daughter harder. Thank God he hadn't given into his baser instincts and gone across to Hallie's cottage.

"You did exactly the right thing. We can't have secrets in this house or Paul's never going to get better. Let's go."

He grabbed his clothes and raced after her.

Before they reached Paul's suite of rooms on the next floor, Vincent could hear his heart wrenching sobs. They took him back to the time when Arlette had first threatened to kill their unborn child.

After begging her not to do anything, Vincent had run outside to the vineyard in agony. For a good part of the night the sobs had poured out of him. When morning came, he'd gone to Pere for help.

His son needed help now.

With his arm around his daughter, he knocked on the door. "Paul? We have to talk. Open up, or I'll be forced to take the door off the hinges."

They waited a good five minutes before Vincent heard the click of the lock. He pushed the door open.

His wreck of a son had found the nearest chair. He sat there with legs apart, head down in an attitude of abject misery.

Vincent drew in a labored breath. "There's nothing in this life we can't forgive if there's enough love, Paul. Whatever it is that's tearing you apart, you can tell me."

Slowly Paul lifted his head. "I'm a liar, Papa."

"Join the club."

He tried to blink the tears away. "This is serious."

"All lies are serious. How about the one I let you believe about your mother?"

"But you had a good reason. You didn't want Monique and me to think badly of her." Vincent couldn't believe what he was hearing. "My lie is different."

"In what way?" he prodded. The suspense made Vincent feel like he was going to jump out of his skin. Monique stood at his side, waiting and trembling.

"I never had a death wish."

When the words sank in, Vincent's joy left him feeling lightheaded.

"I wasn't trying to take my life—the reason I got hit was because I was angry and didn't watch where I was going."

"I *knew* it!" Monique declared. "You lied to the doctor to prevent Hallie from leaving France."

Paul nodded, then looked up sheepishly at Vincent. "I also wanted to make you feel horrible for not listening to me."

"None of that matters now." In the next instant he grabbed hold of his son and gave him a bear hug.

Just when Vincent thought maybe he was about to see light at the end of the tunnel Paul said, "There's something else I have to tell both of you."

Suddenly there was another pit in Vincent's stomach. "Hallie's gone."

Vincent staggered under the revelation.

"Where?" Monique's cry resounded in the bedroom.

"Back to Paris. It's my fault."

A moan escaped Vincent's lips prompting his ever observant daughter to exclaim, "Papa? Are you all right? You look as pale as a ghost."

"It's probably the shock of so many surprises in one night," he muttered before sitting down on the end of Paul's bed. "Tell us what happened."

A bleak look entered his son's eyes. "After I picked her up, I did another terrible thing."

"Go on."

"I accused her of sleeping with you."

That was a new bombshell, one Vincent hadn't been expecting. But when he remembered the strange look on Paul's face at the moment Vincent had come out of Hallie's cottage earlier in the day, it all started to make sense.

Monique remained strangely quiet. He watched her sink down on the chair with her head bowed.

"I knew it wasn't true," Paul confessed, "but after Louis said he'd seen you and Hallie at the river—you know how he can be when he thinks there's something going on—it got to me."

Vincent knew exactly how Louis could be, and Michel, and a dozen others just like them.

"Is that what made Hallie leave St. Genes? The gossip?" Vincent inquired, trying to sound normal when he was dying inside.

"No." Paul paced the floor, then stopped and swung around. "I told her that even if nothing had happened between you two yet, it was only a matter of time." After a hesitation, "I told her to get out of my life.

"She said she would as soon I took her home to pack because her mission here in St. Genes had been accomplished." He groaned. "There was no stopping her—

"At the train station she admitted that she loved me like the brother who'd died in that plane crash. Then she begged me to let you help me, Papa. It wasn't till that moment I realized she still thought I'd tried to kill myself.

"I ran after her to tell her the truth, but I couldn't catch up to her." Tears ran down his face. "I've really screwed things up."

Vincent was too devastated to think, but he had to do something to help his son out of this morass.

"What would you like to do about it?"

"Go to her and apologize for putting her through hell. The only trouble is, she said she'd be unavailable."

By now his daughter was shedding not-so-silent tears.

"Maybe you could put your thoughts in a letter and send it to the abbey by overnight courier."

"She probably wouldn't open it." But Vincent noticed his son hadn't negated his suggestion out of hand.

"If you can say that about Hallie, you don't know her at all!" Monique's pain drove her from the bedroom.

There were degrees of pain. Vincent could say with absolute certitude he was acquainted with them all.

CHAPTER NINE

"Do you have some place go, Hallie?"

"Yes, Holy Mother. My friend in San Diego is going to let me stay with her until I can find an apartment of my own. Hopefully there's enough time before fall to obtain a teaching job in one of the public schools."

Mother Marie-Claire smiled at Hallie. "Some women take their vows, then find out too late there's something else they would rather do. I'm glad you're not one of them. I think you're wise and courageous because you've faced the truth about yourself in time.

"You may not be a lay nun anymore, but like Sister Carlotta, you will always be a strong force wherever your road takes you. I have no doubt of it."

"I hope so."

"When is your flight?"

"In the morning."

"We'll always keep you in our prayers."

"Thank you for everything, Holy Mother."

Hallie got up to leave her office. On the way out the door, the mistress of novices approached her. She had two express mail packages in her hand.

"These were just delivered to the abbey. They're both for you."

"*Merci.*"

She tucked them under her arm and left the convent to go for a walk along the Seine. Gaby had probably sent her some money or something. It was the kind of generous thing her friend would do. Hard to believe that within forty-eight hours she'd be holding Gaby's little girl for the first time.

As soon as Hallie found an unoccupied bench, she sat down in the warm noon day sun and looked at the first envelope. When she saw that it had originated from St. Genes, she let out a little cry of surprise.

A quick check of the second envelope showed it had been sent from Pully. That was the town where she'd gone with Vincent. Had he sent this? Her heart thudded until it hurt.

Deciding to save it until last, she opened the first one and pulled out a white envelope. Inside was a one page letter written on the computer from Paul.

She wept for happiness to learn he'd lied about wanting to die. After he'd apologized profusely for everything, her gaze fastened on the last paragraph.

I hope this reaches you before you leave for California. I guess it's too much to hope you might come back to Chateau Rolland. If you'll give me a second chance, I promise things will be different this time. Just remember you've got a younger brother here who will always love you.

"*Paul*—" she whispered his name. Her eyes closed tightly. One of her prayers had been answered.

With trembling hands she opened the second envelope. Her spirits were dashed when she discovered it was a one page letter, hand-written, from Monique.

What a foolish foolish girl Hallie was to think it might have been from Vincent. Not that she didn't want to hear from Monique. Hallie adored her, but...

Hallie—
No one has any idea I'm writing to you. By now you've already read Paul's letter and know about the

terrible lie he told to everyone.

You have to come back! I'm not saying that he's going to kill himself if you don't. We both have proof he won't. But I know Paul better than anyone in this world. He'll be sad all his life for the things he said and did to you if you don't give him an opportunity to repent.

I had a talk with Father Olivier about everything. He says it's even more important for the person who has been sinned against to help the repentant sinner fully repent. Paul can't do that if you're not here.

Do you want that on your conscience when you join the convent? I should think not.

Monique.

Hallie put the letter down on the bench and stared into space. She could picture Monique stamping her well shod foot as she took Hallie to task.

The little monkey had actually gone to Father Olivier. It wrenched Hallie's heart because she could feel the love and the pleading behind Monique's missive.

Something told Hallie that if she didn't go back, even if it was just for a few days, Monique might end up more injured than Paul would ever be. That wouldn't be fair to Vincent who'd had enough pain to last him several lifetimes.

With her mind made up, Hallie gathered the letters and started for the abbey. She would have to phone Gaby and tell her why she was putting her plans to return to San Diego on hold for a short while. After that she would cancel her airline reservation and make one for the train.

It was 10:30 p.m. when Hallie's train pulled into the station at St. Genes. Close to eleven the taxi drove

Hallie around the back of the chateau to her cottage. The twins' cars were parked in the courtyard. She didn't see Vincent's in either the front or the back.

Neither of his children had mentioned him in their letters. It could mean anything or nothing, yet the fact that he was out late again tended to make Hallie believe he was seeing another woman.

Why not? It would be the most natural thing in the world, especially now that he knew his son wasn't suicidal and never had been. If her own reaction to Paul's confession was anything to go by, Vincent's relief had to be exquisite.

"Merci, monsieur." Hallie paid the chauffeur and got out of the taxi with her suitcase.

Since Paul had her key in his car, she was forced to go next door to the other cottage and ask Bernard for the spare. Thankfully he hadn't gone to bed yet and obliged her without question.

If he wondered where she'd been the last few days, he didn't say anything, only that he'd bring over some fresh towels.

Her apartment was exactly as she'd left it three nights ago. No one had been in it, or if they had, the fridge hadn't been cleaned out yet. It surprised her to feel this much at home when she'd only lived in it for a day or two.

Maybe it was the thrill of being back. All she knew was that her appetite had come back. She walked back to the kitchen to fix herself a ham and cheese omelet. The fruit she and Vincent had picked out in the open air market still looked good.

As she bit into a pear which was incredibly sweet to

the taste, vivid memories of the unforgettable afternoon they'd spent together assailed her.

This was the part that was going to be hard—to be around Vincent again and keep all her longings for him suppressed. But for the twins' sake, for Monique's in particular, Hallie had to do it.

She'd just taken her food to the dining room when she heard a rap on the door. Putting everything down, she hurried to the foyer and opened it thinking it was Bernard.

A gasp escaped her throat to see Vincent's tall, powerful body standing there in a black silk shirt and gray trousers. He smelled wonderful. The man looked so— he looked so incredibly handsome, she almost fainted in reaction.

"Hallie…"

He sounded and acted equally shocked to discover her on the premises. Apparently she was the last person in the world he'd expected to see again. In a familiar gesture she knew he wasn't aware of, she watched his hand rub the back of his neck.

"I saw lights on and came to investigate."

She moistened her dry lips nervously. "Yes, well the taxi just brought me from the train. As it was so late and I didn't want to disturb anyone, I thought I'd wait until tomorrow to let your family know I'd returned."

Like someone brailling another person from head to toe, his dark eyes went everywhere. If he'd had his hands on her, the effect would have been the same. Her legs started to tremble.

"For how long?" he demanded in what sounded like a hoarse whisper.

Her heart was pounding out of control. "I'm not really sure."

It was the truth. Vincent didn't know it, but he held all the answers.

The compelling male mouth she was dying to feel on her own, thinned into a hard uncompromising line. It darkened his whole countenance.

"Then why did you come back at all?" She heard rebuke in his gruff query.

"Come in and I'll explain."

No sooner had he stepped over the threshold than Bernard showed up. Vincent took the towels from him and came all the way inside, shutting the door behind him with his foot.

He tossed them on the nearest chair, then put his hands on his hips in a totally masculine stance. Vincent wanted an answer. She couldn't blame him, not after the trauma they'd lived through.

"Just a minute. I have something to show you that will explain everything."

She dashed to the bedroom and opened her suitcase. The two letters sat on top of her clothes. Without wasting a second, she hurried back to the salon where she found him pacing the floor.

He put her in mind of a gorgeous black panther going round and round the bars of his cage, looking for some avenue of escape.

Hallie intended to give him one. He stopped moving when he saw her.

"Read Paul's letter first." She handed it to him.

He took it from her, but his eyes had narrowed on her face. "You mean there's more than one?"

She nodded. "Your daughter's."

A stillness seemed to surround him. "Monique wrote to you, too?" He sounded incredulous.

Since sending his children to school in Paris, Vincent

had met with many shocks and surprises. They just kept coming, and it was all because of Hallie.

She waited anxiously while he read their letters.

He must have reached the part in Monique's that had gotten to Hallie because his head reared back unexpectedly.

"When my daughter said she would drive to the church and explain to Father Olivier that you'd been called back to Paris on an emergency, I had no idea there was another agenda motivating her."

His eyes clouded in disappointment. "Monique stepped over the line, Hallie. I'm sorry she went to these lengths to play on your guilt. I obviously don't know her as well as I thought I did."

"Don't be upset with her," Hallie begged him. "She needed help and went to someone she trusted."

Vincent let out a sound of frustration. "She should have come to me."

"How could she do that when she knew you would forbid her to bother me?"

They stared at each other for a long, unsmiling moment. He couldn't respond to that because he knew she'd spoken the truth.

"I have to tell you something about your daughter, Vincent. She's an expert observer of human nature and has been studying you for years. There's very little that gets by her."

The taut line of his mouth softened. "Tell me about it."

Relieved to see that he wasn't quite as upset as before Hallie said, "Father Olivier was right you know. My coming back here to stay for a while will prove to Paul I received his letter, and most importantly, that I've forgiven him."

Vincent eyed her with a penetrating glance. "This won't work if he learns about Monique's letter."

"Then I'll destroy the evidence."

She took the letters from his hand and walked to the kitchen. There was a box of matches on top of the stove. She reached for it.

"Let me," he murmured. Within seconds they both watched the papers curl against the lick of flame. Those precious letters whose words were inscribed in her heart.

He washed the debris down the kitchen sink.

Fearing he would go she said, "Are you hungry?" Hallie couldn't stand the thought of his leaving. Not yet...

"A-as you can see, I just fixed me an omelet and haven't put anything away yet," she stammered. "I could make one for you if you'd like."

She held her breath, afraid to look at him.

"That would be fine, but only if you let me fix it."

"That's fine," she said, struggling to sound unaffected. "I'll go get mine from the dining room and reheat it."

They worked side by side in harmony. She loved the way he pitched in to do whatever was needed. He broke half a dozen eggs into the pan.

"You must be hungry."

Even if he'd been out to dinner earlier with a woman, like most men he still seemed to have room for more. The thought of him having just come from a clinging pair of feminine arms killed her.

"I am now."

What did he mean? That her return had brought him back to life? If only he knew that being alone with him like this made her thankful she was alive.

"When you attend as many business dinners as I do, food's the last thing you care about. If Paul or Monique decide they want to be an active part of the business one day, I'll gladly turn over the duty dinners to them."

His answer thrilled her.

"It'll be interesting to see what path their lives take once they've been to college."

"Let's hope that whatever they choose, it will make them happy."

Was that regret she heard in his voice?

She eyed him with curiosity. "If you could have done anything else, what would it have been?"

"There was a time when I thought I'd like to go into medicine, but my father wouldn't hear of it."

Hallie could see Vincent as a doctor. Someone caring and dedicated.

He flicked her searching glance. "Did you always know you wanted to be a teacher?" By now they'd taken their food to the table.

"Pretty much. However my motivation stemmed more from having my summers and holidays free to travel. The teaching part was harder than I had anticipated."

"My children think you're brilliant."

"The twins are full of it, as we say in America."

His expression grew sober. "In all seriousness, their English has vastly improved being around you. Being under your influence was the best thing that could have happened to them. When I think of the way I spoke to you at my apartment—"

His hand reached for hers and squeezed it. "Forgive me, Hallie."

"We've been through all this before." Her voice

came out sounding shaky. "There's nothing to forgive."

She wished he would pull her right onto his lap. Instead, he let her go and finished eating. Hallie didn't know what to make of all the mixed signals she was getting.

"Now that you're here, we'd better return to things as they were. Paul won't be convinced unless everything gets back to normal. Why don't you come to my office at nine in the morning and I'll put you to work."

Hallie was so excited at the prospect of being with him during the day, she almost dropped her fork.

"I think that would be for the best."

She drained the glass of grape juice he'd poured for her. Since he knew she didn't drink wine, he'd thoughtfully provided a substitute. Everything he did caused her to fall deeper and deeper in love with him.

"When I see Monique at breakfast, I'll tell her to let Father Olivier know you'll be teaching those English classes after all."

"Good," she murmured. "When you talk to her, would you mind asking her if I can use one of her bikes to get around?"

He eyed her speculatively. "If you need transportation, you can always take my car."

On that note he sank his white teeth into a juicy plum. She decided it was his favorite fruit.

"That's very generous, but I need the exercise. When I was in my teens and dreamed of going on great adventures, I used to imagine myself cycling through France.

"Being here at the chateau surrounded by miles of beautiful vineyards is like a dream come true. I don't want to miss a second of it," her voice trembled.

In the silence that followed, a change seemed to come over him. His jaw hardened perceptibly.

"You mean before you find yourself in a third world country teaching the impoverished while your body is unsuccessfully fighting off parasites?"

His anger was so stunning, it caught Hallie off guard.

She'd been planning to tell him she was no longer a lay nun, that she wouldn't be going to South America. It was a matter of finding the right time, when it came up naturally in the conversation.

It *had* come up naturally in the conversation.

But there was a problem if the knowledge that she was free to live a normal life turned out to be a big turnoff for him.

Hallie wasn't naive. She knew he found her attractive. A man's eyes didn't lie. But even taking Paul out of the equation, that attraction might have been prolonged because she represented forbidden fruit.

What if he thought she'd given up a religious life for him? Once he learned he could pluck it from the tree and have all he wanted, would he lose his desire for it?

There had to have been other women in his life who'd hoped to be the next Madame Rolland. So far it hadn't happened. It seemed he was content with his life the way it was.

If he'd sent Hallie a letter along with the children's— Or if he'd tried to reach her by phone on behalf of his children— If he'd shown any little extra sign that he wanted her, she wouldn't be having these doubts now.

Her feelings were so raw she feared that once she informed him she was no longer a lay nun, she'd end up blurting that she loved him. It would crush her if he didn't return her feelings.

In a surprise move, he pushed himself away from the

table and stood up. The action tipped her empty glass over. It startled her so much her eyes flicked to his in astonishment.

He seemed to be out of breath. "Forgive me, Hallie. I have no right to question anything about your future. It's enough that you've returned to help the twins adjust."

She watched him rake a suntanned hand through his hair.

"Make no mistake. Monique's letter was a desperate ploy to keep you in her life." His eyes looked haunted. "She adores you."

"I'm crazy about her, too," Hallie admitted.

"I never thought I'd say this, but I'm hoping she meets a young man this summer who'll become important enough to take away the sting of your departure."

Will you feel the sting, too? Tell me, Vincent, her heart cried.

"It's getting late. I'm sure you're tired after your train ride. I'll let myself out."

His long strides ate up the distance to the front door. Then he was gone.

More than anything in the world she wanted to call him back and tell him what was in her heart, but she didn't have the courage.

She was waiting for a sign.

Maybe a few days more and one would come.

"Pere? Are you awake?" The bedroom was dark.

"No. Come in."

Vincent's grandfather lay in the double bed listening to the radio. It was his ritual before falling asleep. Beauregard slept next to him.

The dog raised his head, made a little moan of greeting, then put his head down again.

The old man turned on the lamp. Vincent drew up a chair next to him.

A pair of dark wise old eyes scrutinized him. "Eighteen years ago you came to this room to tell me Arlette was going to do away with your unborn child and you wanted my help to stop her.

"Tonight there's an air about you that tells me you want my help again. But this time it's about Hallie Linn if I'm not mistaken."

Vincent nodded. "She came back tonight, but it's only temporary."

After he'd told his grandfather about the letters, the old man said, "Unfortunately there's no attorney on earth who can stop her from becoming a nun."

"Don't you think I know that?" Vincent cried out in pain.

"Be still for a moment." The gnarled fingers which had worked too many years with the vines gripped Vincent's arm. "I said no attorney, but the love of a good man could."

Vincent buried his face in his hands.

"Love for your children has brought Hallie back to St. Genes a second time. Is it so impossible to believe she might love you, too?"

"But would it be enough to dissuade her from her vocation?" A shudder rocked Vincent's body. "I couldn't take it if she turned me down."

"What's the difference between that hell and the one you're living in now? Are you going to sit there crippled by Arlette's evil and lose out on the greatest chance at happiness a man could wish for?"

"It isn't just that."

"You're talking about Paul."

Vincent shot out of the chair, disturbing the dog. "We've resolved everything between us, but if he had any idea—"

"Then go to him and tell him what you're feeling."

"I can't take that risk."

His grandfather gazed at him with sad eyes. "I'm sorry there isn't anything I can do."

"Yes, there is. Stay alive for me."

Vincent left his grandfather's bedroom and headed down the hall toward one of the drawing rooms where he entertained guests who came to the chateau on business. Etvige kept the bar well stocked.

The last time Vincent could remember drinking himself into a stupor was the night he'd learned that Arlette would never be able to hurt him or his children again. The joy he'd felt on that occasion had given him cause to celebrate.

Tonight he would welcome the same oblivion to take away his pain for a few hours.

After finding an unopened bottle of scotch, he raced up the staircase to his bedroom eager to feel its numbing effect.

The first glass went down in one gulp.

The second one never made it to his lips because Paul had come into his bedroom unannounced. He was still dressed in jeans and a T-shirt.

"I thought you would have been asleep long ago."

"Me, too, but Pere didn't feel well after dinner and went to bed early. It worried me."

Vincent didn't know about that because he'd been to a vintners' dinner meeting in St. Emilion. He put the glass of scotch on the table. "I was just with him. He never said a word."

Paul stood there with his hands in his back pockets. "I know. It turns out he had indigestion. Etvige gave him something for it before you got home.

"A little while ago I decided to check up on him one more time and take Beauregard out. That's when I heard the two of you talking."

Warmth filled Vincent's neck and face. Part of it was the scotch, but not all of it.

"Why didn't you come all the way in and let us know you were there?"

"Because I found out something I've suspected from the moment you brought Hallie to the hospital." He started shaking his head. "It's obvious you two have been fighting your attraction for each other since the very beginning.

"I saw it and felt it, but I didn't want to believe it because I'd found Hallie first."

Vincent hadn't drunk enough scotch to dull the effect of this newly inflicted pain.

"Paul—"

"It's all right. Hallie never saw me as anything but a brother substitute. I made a complete and utter ass of myself over her, but it's all in the past now. That's what I'm trying to tell you.

"The night the guys came over to the chateau, Luc told me afterward he could see you and Hallie had the hots for each other." Vincent winced. "That was no news to me.

"Papa—if she decides not to enter the convent, I hope you two end up together. You're really good for each other. Why do you think I wrote her that letter? I'm assuming she came back to St. Genes tonight because she couldn't stay away from you."

"I'm sure that's the reason, Papa."

To Vincent's shock, his daughter had come in the bedroom. He wondered how long she'd been listening at the door.

"I wrote Hallie a letter, too, but she couldn't have received it until this morning. How do you account for her not even waiting another day before catching the next train?

"I think it's pretty amazing myself. If I were the holy mother, I'd tell Hallie she wasn't ready to take her vows and never would be."

It *was* amazing. All of it. Absolutely amazing.

Vincent wondered if the scotch was the reason for this fantastic hallucination in which the twins had just given their permission for him to pursue Hallie.

"You're perfect for each other, *mon pere*."

"I agree," Paul declared.

"Is that so."

Vincent put his arms around his children and walked them to the hallway. "I love you both and appreciate all you've said. But the fact remains that Hallie isn't free, and no matter how it looks to you, she might not want to be for reasons we don't know anything about."

Monique fixed him with one of her bold stares. "But you're going to talk to her and find out."

"When the time is right."

She shook her head. "You have to make the time."

"Listen to Monique. She knows what she's talking about," Paul advised, sounding more like the father than the son here. "If you wait, she might get on another train and you'll lose her for good."

Long after everyone had gone to bed, Vincent still lay there wide awake. Paul's warning had put the fear in him.

CHAPTER TEN

HALLIE had been awake since five, waiting for nine o'clock to come so she could be with Vincent.

Time hung so heavy on her hands, she decided it would be a good idea to walk to town and see Father Olivier. When the priest learned she'd put away her plan to be a nun, he might have reservations about her teaching classes to the youth group. She wouldn't blame him if he did.

In any event, her visit wouldn't take long. She'd be back in plenty of time to look in on the twins before she reported for work.

At five after six Hallie left the cottage. She loved the early morning and was glad to get going. It was already warm out. That meant the day would end up being a hot one. Now was the perfect time to fit in some exercise.

With every step she took, the beauty of the Dordogne valley overwhelmed her. The earth, the vines, all the foliage was so lush. There was a fruity scent in the soft air, subtle, yet noticeable.

It was wonderful to be alive. Vincent was the reason for her *joie de vivre*. He made everything about her life exciting and worthwhile.

Was it chance or destiny that had brought her to France?

She wanted to believe it was the latter. When she'd fought against coming here, how could she have known she'd meet a man like him? Bigger than life, yet someone wonderfully real and down to earth.

To have Vincent's love would fulfill her in ways nothing else ever could. To be his wife, to have a baby with him...

The fantasy occupied her thoughts so completely that before she knew it, she'd arrived at the church. As she approached the outer door, she saw the priest coming up the road toward her with a baguette under one arm and a thermos in his other hand.

"Bonjour!" He waved to her.

She waved back and held the door open for him.

"Come in to my office and join me for breakfast."

A minute later he plied her with bread and a cup of hot coffee. He explained that the housekeeper at the rectory made the best brew in all St. Genes.

She watched him soak his bread in the steaming liquid before putting it in his mouth. Then he leaned back in his chair to enjoy it. "Now tell me what was the emergency that took you back to Paris."

Throughout her explanation he kept munching. The only thing she didn't confide was her love for Vincent. When she'd finished, the priest gazed at her for a moment before smiling at her.

"It's clear to me you have something else important to do with your life. One of them is to help my little flock with their English. I'll expect you on Wednesday night at seven."

Her eyes prickled. "Thank you, Father."

She got up from the chair. "Now I'd better get back to the chateau. I'm training for a new job and don't want to be late."

"I'll walk you out. It's too beautiful a morning to stay indoors."

"I agree."

They stepped outside the church in time to see the man she'd been fantasizing about come striding toward them from the parking area. He really was the most attractive male she'd ever laid eyes on.

Hallie's heart hammered too hard and fast to be healthy.

"*Salut,* Vincent!" the priest called to him. "If you've come for Hallie, we've finished our talk and she's ready to go back to the chateau with you."

Vincent said hello to the priest, but something was wrong. She could tell by the rigidity of his body. His dark eyes scrutinized her relentlessly.

"I brought Monique's bike to your cottage this morning. To my surprise I discovered you weren't there."

She pursed her lips. "I'm sorry to have put you out. Thank you for going to the trouble. I'll use it from now on."

Father Olivier patted Vincent's arm. "Hallie was worried I might not let her teach now that she's no longer a lay nun, but I told her the church will always welcome her talents."

Suddenly Hallie heard Vincent say her name under his breath. His eyes kindled until they resembled two dark flames.

The news was out now. She couldn't reclaim the words. She didn't want to.

"You've left the outreach program?"

His deep voice was so unsteady, the revelation came to her that he'd been waiting a long time to hear those words. Possibly for as long as she'd been wanting to say them.

She nodded, afraid to speak until they could be alone.

"Let's go."

The urgency of those words thrilled her to the center of her being. Hallie murmured goodbye to the priest and started for the car ahead of him. She didn't dare let Vincent touch her yet.

Seconds later he joined her in the front seat. He didn't say anything. Instead he grasped the hand closest to him and raised it to his lips. When he kissed her palm, her body shook with needs she could no longer control.

Without letting go, he turned on the motor and drove them over the bridge leading out of town. She knew exactly where he was taking her. Her desire for him was so great, she feared she might just have to climb onto his lap before they got there.

The moment the car stopped at the river's edge, he pulled her body into his arms.

Her name came out on a fierce whisper as he cradled her head between his hands. She felt his warm breath on her mouth. A hot, sweet sensation invaded her limbs.

"Vincent—"

Her breathing grew shallow as his dark face drew closer. Then his mouth closed possessively over hers and coherent thought ceased to exist. Time had no meaning as they attempted to satisfy their insatiable hunger for each other.

This was the moment she'd been born for, had been waiting for.

Filled with an all-consuming need, she wrapped her arms around his neck, desperate to show this incredible man what he meant to her. She was prepared to give him anything and everything.

Delirious with longing, she kissed him endlessly, craving the ecstasy he aroused in her.

"I love you, darling," she whispered over and over

again against his lips and cheeks and eyes and hair. "You can't imagine how much."

It was marvelous to feel alive again. To feel loved.

Hallie kept making little moaning sounds as she drowned in the sensations he created with every touch of his hands and mouth.

His beautiful, enticing male mouth. She would never be able to get enough of it. Not in a lifetime.

Vincent buried his face in her hair.

"I'm in love with you, Hallie. I'm in so deep, it's forever. As far as I'm concerned, you've just made your final vows to me. There's no going back. I need you too much," his voice shook before they were devouring each other again.

His mouth was sealed over hers with smothering force until she was a quivering mass of emotion and desire.

"You're mine now, *mon amour.*"

The French endearment thrilled her.

"I *want* to be yours! That's why I returned," she cried against his lips. "There's no life without *you.*"

"Hallie, Hallie." He pressed hot kisses against the side of her neck. "I never dreamed that at the point my own children were standing on the brink of adulthood, I would come across the great love of my life. It never occurred to me it could happen now.

"Yet look at me! I'm trembling like a schoolboy. You've made me feel young again, like I could do anything again. I don't recognize myself anymore. It's all because of you. Kiss me again to let me know this is real."

Hallie willingly complied. Vincent was her life. What heaven to be in his arms in this paradisiacal spot of earth where they could love each other into oblivion.

Much later he moved his head. "I'm only upset with my son for one thing," he murmured on a ragged breath against her mouth. "That he didn't introduce us the first time I came to see the twins in Paris. Because he kept you a secret, we've missed months and months of living and loving."

"I know," her voice throbbed. "I've thought about that, too. I'm thinking about it now." She swallowed hard and buried her face in his neck. "You realize we're going to go through a lot more pain when we tell Paul that we're in love."

Hallie didn't understand when she heard a sound like joy escape his throat.

"*Mon amour*—I've been so on fire for you, I haven't told you what you need to hear."

"What?" She lifted her head so she could look into those velvety brown eyes that burned for her.

"Paul has given us his blessing."

She shook her head, wanting it to be true. "When?"

"Last night."

In the next breath he told her about the conversation with his children after he'd walked out of the cottage.

Her relief was so great, she broke down sobbing. "He's really all right with it?" She still couldn't quite believe it.

"I understand how shocked you must be. I felt the same way. But there was a sincerity about him. Paul truly has grown up. I saw a light in his eyes, and knew then. He wants us to be together."

"Oh, Vincent—" she grabbed hold of him and clung. "I've never been this happy in the whole of my life. I love your children. Being with them always felt right. They love their papa.

"They made me love him, too. All I had to do was

172 THE FRENCHMAN'S BRIDE

meet you in person and *'voilà—'* as your adorable daughter always says, I fell head over heels in love with you.''

Vincent's groan of pleasure came from deep within his throat. He pressed kisses to the scented hollow of hers. ''The whole time you were telling me off in my own apartment, I recognized something profound was happening to me.

''No matter how I raged, you came back with irrefutable truths that tied me in knots and confounded me until I knew my life would never be the same again.

''If Paul hadn't ended up in the hospital, I would have come after you that night to apologize. There's no way I would have let you get away from me.''

''I'm ashamed to say I didn't want to get away from you, either. Despite the crisis with Paul, when I saw you waiting for me outside Tati's, I swear my legs almost gave away from excitement.''

She stared into his eyes. ''But the real moment of truth came to me when we drove in to the estate and Monique jumped out of the car to run to Pere.

''I kept thinking 'this feels right. This feels like home to me.' I got out of the car and started walking through the vines because it all seemed familiar.''

''Like it was meant to be?'' he said in a husky voice. ''Yes.''

''I had the same feeling as I watched you walk toward my family. My breath caught because I could imagine you being there and doing that for the rest of our lives.

''It was the defining moment for me…my twins and the remarkable woman they'd brought home to St. Genes. If I didn't know it then, I know it now. A force greater than all of us set the stage for our meeting, Hallie.''

She nodded, burying her face against his shoulder once more.

''We need you, *mon amour*.'' His whole body was shaking with emotion. He kissed her hair. ''All of us. Even Pere whose life you've already touched in ways you can't imagine.

''His birthday is July the second. Shall we make that our wedding day? It'll be the greatest gift we could ever give him. He's helped me get through this life with fear and trembling.

''I want to give him the one thing that will bring him happiness and peace in his old age. Marriage to you.''

''What a beautiful thing to say,'' she cried. ''That's what I want, darling. To be your wife. I want your babies.''

He covered her face in kisses. ''I've been thinking about that, too.''

''Vincent?'' She sat up straighter. ''Am I going too fast for you?''

''Too fast?'' He burst into laughter. ''Don't you know I saw a couple of blond toddlers trailing behind you in the vineyard during my own personal vision?''

A smile broke out on her face. ''A couple?''

He nodded. ''Twins run in my mother's family.''

''You're kidding!'' The thought filled her with wonder. ''I wonder how Paul and Monique would feel about that?''

''Shall we go home and find out? I have no doubts my daughter will tell us exactly what she thinks. In fact she'll want to plan our wedding. Do you mind?''

Hallie kissed the corner of his mouth. ''You know better than that. I can't imagine anything more wonderful. She organized all our outings. Everything went off without a hitch. Monique's a born leader. Whatever she ends up doing in this life, she'll be the head of it."

A lazy grin broke out on his handsome face. "That's my daughter." His fingers played with one errant blond curl. "What's really miraculous is that you know and understand her so well. She's very particular about the people she lets into her life."

"Is that one of the reasons why you didn't marry again?"

"No. There's only one reason I never married. I was waiting for you."

"Vincent—"

As his mouth closed over hers and their passion grew, they heard a horn honk. He wrenched his lips from hers with a groan.

"We're beginning to attract the interest of the locals. Let's go back to your cottage where we can be alone. Much as I love it here, this is no place for what I have in mind for the two of us."

Heat crept into her cheeks.

With the greatest of reluctance she moved back to her side of the car. Hoping there was a mirror, she put down the visor to look at herself and try to repair the damage.

She let out a small gasp when she saw how flushed she was. Her lips looked swollen from his kisses. His hands had disheveled her hair, and her eyes shone like stars. Anyone seeing her would know what she'd been doing.

Vincent started up the car, but he didn't take his eyes off her.

"In case I haven't told you yet, you're infinitely beautiful to me, inside and out."

She reached for his hand and didn't let go for the short journey home. It was after two when they drove through the gates of the estate. Though they'd spent hours at the river, being with Vincent had seemed but a moment. To think this was only the beginning.

As they drew closer to the chateau she saw movement in the courtyard. "It's the twins—they're riding bikes. Those little monkeys. They must know you went looking for me."

"We gave them quite a wait didn't we."

Memories of their passionate interlude bathed her in fresh warmth. She turned to Vincent. "I'm sorry I walked to church and ruined your plans for us."

He moved his hand to her thigh and squeezed it gently. "I'm not. If you hadn't gone to see the priest, I might still be trying to break you down and force a confession of love from you."

"You wouldn't have had to use force. After being with you last night, I couldn't have held out any longer."

"That's nice to hear because it looks like my children can't wait any longer to find out if anything significant has gone on between us. Let's play dumb till we're inside your cottage."

"Vincent Rolland—you *can* be a tease!" she exclaimed.

"What do you mean?"

"Your son is one of the biggest teases I know. I decided he didn't get that trait from you. Now I'm not so sure."

He eyed her with a decidedly devilish look. "There are still a few things about me you have yet to learn."

She tried to breathe and couldn't. "I can't wait, darling."

"Neither can I."

The twins followed them to the cottage.

Vincent's eyes flashed Hallie a private message of love as he helped her from the car.

Monique parked her bike and put down the kickstand. "Hallie! I was hoping you'd come back!" She hurried toward her.

Hallie's heart melted to feel Monique's arms go around her. Paul looked on with a nervous smile.

After letting go of his sister, Hallie reached for him and gave him a long, hard hug. "When I read your letter, I had to come back. Don't say you're sorry anymore. The misunderstandings are behind us. You and Monique are my two favorite people in the world. I love you."

"I love you, too, Hallie." He sounded choked up. "Please say you're going to stay for the rest of the summer." The hope in his voice was all she needed to hear.

It was a good thing he couldn't look in her eyes right then. "I am. I've made the necessary arrangements."

"That's terrific!"

When he moved away from her, she could see the nervousness he'd been feeling was gone.

Vincent stood there eyeing his children. "I'm glad someone got use out of those bikes today. As usual, Hallie was up at the crack of dawn and didn't wait for transportation. I found her at the church getting around on her own two feet."

"She's a busy bee, Papa."

Their father grinned. "You two sound so American, I hardly know you anymore." After a pause, "Have you had lunch?"

Paul shook his head. "We were waiting to eat with you."

Hallie got the key out of her purse. "Then come on in and I'll fix us something. Father Olivier shared his breakfast with me but that was a long time ago."

By tacit agreement everyone moved inside.

The place hummed with activity as Vincent's family got in the act putting fruit and drinks on the table. Hallie pulled the extra ham and cheese croissants from the fridge and warmed them in the oven. Without fresh French bread, she couldn't make sandwiches.

"Has anyone seen Pere today?" Vincent asked once they'd started to eat.

"I ate breakfast with him," Paul said. "He's over at the plant right now."

"Good. That means he's all right after his bout of indigestion."

Paul nodded.

"I've been thinking about Pere. With his eighty-eighth birthday coming up, I thought we ought to plan something really special."

Hallie's heart started to pick up speed and refused to slow down.

Monique darted her father a puzzled glance. "We always have a nice party for him."

"I realize that, petite. But this year I'm thinking of inviting friends and business people from Europe and the U.S. as well as the locals."

His daughter's eyes flickered with interest. "You're talking about a huge reception!" She sounded excited.

"Yes. Do you think Pere would like that, Paul?"

"Sure. Sometimes when he's melancholy, he talks about the way it used to be years ago when Mamie was alive and they had big parties here."

"Good. Then it's settled. We'll have to get the invitations out this week. July second will be here before we know it."

"We'll send engraved announcements on heavy crème paper using the chateau's logo," Monique began thinking outloud. "For the wording let's put, you are cordially invited to celebrate with us on the occasion of Pierre Maurice Rolland's eighty-eighth birthday.

"Let's see—" She thought for a moment. "Seven p.m. until ten p.m., le deux juillet, chez le Chateau Roland, St. Genes, France."

Vincent eyed his daughter with a decided gleam.

The suspense was almost too much for Hallie.

"I only have a few things to add, *mignonne,* otherwise it's perfect."

Monique looked at her father in surprise. "What else could there be?"

His gaze slid to Hallie's, blinding her with his love.

"It needs a comma after birthday followed by, *and the marriage of Jean-Vincent Rolland to Ms. Hallie Linn of Bel Air, California. No gifts please.*"

There was a collective silence followed by a collective cry.

"Papa!"

EPILOGUE

Le Chateau Rolland
July 2, two years later

HALLIE could hear her fussy daughter even before Anne-Marie, Minou's cousin, knocked on the outer door of the master bedroom. "Pardon, Hallie, but Catherine refuses to go down until her maman comes to kiss her goodnight."

She sprayed herself with some Fleurs de Rocailles. "I'll be right there, Anne-Marie."

Guests would be arriving any minute to honor Pere on his ninetieth birthday. She and Vincent were celebrating their second wedding anniversary at the same time.

He'd already dressed and gone downstairs with Max Calder, Gaby's husband, to join Pere in the study before the crush began.

With her body still trembling from the kisses her husband had given her neck and throat before disappearing, Hallie slipped on the black crepe de chine dress with the cap sleeves and round neck. It had simple lines, but Monique, who'd gone shopping with Hallie a few days ago, had insisted that with her light gold hair, the dress's color and style looked sensational on her.

"Papa will have a heart attack when he sees you in this."

It was another of those American expressions Monique had picked up as tour guide around the cha-

teau and estate each summer. The words had made
Hallie blush.

"I don't want him to have a heart attack," she'd
murmured back. "I want him to stay alive forever! For
moi!"

Monique had given her that shrewd look out of those
soulful brown eyes. "I know. Everyone knows!"

"Am I that bad?"

Her twenty-year-old stepdaughter had grinned.
"You're worse! Whenever you see my father, your eyes
light up like big huge aquamarines and you go all
breathless. No husband in the whole of France has such
an adoring wife. I'm afraid it has gone to his head."

Then she'd hugged Hallie and whispered, "Papa has
needed your love. I never knew he could be this happy.
I thank heaven for you every night."

"I feel the same way about you and the rest of the
family. But if anything, I'm afraid it's your father who
has gone to *my* head." It had happened the moment
they'd met at his apartment in Paris.

Since then, life had been like some fantastic dream
from which she prayed never to awake.

A last brush through her naturally curly blond hair
which she wore a little longer than before, and she was
ready.

The second she reached the corridor, Catherine
lunged toward her, clutching her tiny arms around
Hallie's neck. Anne Marie let out a cry of surprise before they both laughed.

With her daughter clinging to her, Hallie hurried into
the nursery next door where she could hear her son
Jean-Marc's protestations at having been left alone.

The golden-blond one year old twins, named after
Vincent's father and Hallie's mother, had sensed ex-

citement in the air all day and had been exceptionally demanding and restless.

Like Monique and Paul, the babies had inherited Vincent's gorgeous dark brown eyes. Hallie's heart melted to see Jean-Marc standing in his crib crying for her with alligator tears rolling down his flushed cheeks.

"It's all right. Mommy's here." She kissed the top of his head, then put Catherine in her crib. That started another fountain gushing.

After giving her a kiss, she turned to Anne-Marie. "I'm sorry to leave you like this. I'll turn on their favorite musical toy. It plays four tunes over and over. They'll settle down after I go. Just turn out the lights and stay by them for a while."

"Do not worry. Tonight is for you to enjoy with your husband."

She gave Anne-Marie a hug. "Thank you for helping. On special occasions like this, I don't know what we'd do without you."

At times like this Hallie marveled that Vincent had raised his first set of twins on his own. Though he'd had Pere's help, it couldn't have been easy. More than ever she realized what a remarkable man she'd married.

Remarkable and wonderful in so many ways, there was no end to them. No end to the love she felt for him.

After one last look at her precious children, Hallie hurried down the hall to the suite of rooms where they'd put Gaby and Max who'd brought their little dark-haired Hallie with them.

Max was crazy about his wife and adorable daughter. Since they'd come to St. Genes, he walked around with a continual grin because Gaby was expecting their second child in September.

Hallie could hear little Hallie's crying long before she reached the door to their suite. Just then Gaby, looking stunning in black silk, came out of it with a slightly frantic expression on her face. "Poor Minou. I don't know if she's going to quiet down or not. Max stayed with her until Vincent came to get him."

"Don't worry. Minou's wonderful with children. So's Anne-Marie. If there's a problem, one of them will come and find us."

"You're right." Gaby took a calming breath. Her gaze traveled over Hallie.

"Do you remember that time in San Diego when I was working for Girls' Village? We both wore pretend nun's habits to canvas an apartment building."

"How could I ever forget," Hallie said as they walked arm and arm toward the grand staircase.

"I thought I'd never seen anything as beautiful as the sight of you in that nun's outfit the holy mother let you borrow for a disguise. But tonight, I have to tell you, you're absolutely radiant. You made the right choice, Hal."

They started down the stairs.

"I know I did. I haven't had one regret. As wise old Pere once told Monique, 'A man and a woman are doing God's work when they raise a good family.'"

"He was right."

"If I hadn't met Vincent…"

"But you did, just like I met Max. Sometimes I'm so happy it frightens me."

"You're not the only one," Hallie's voice shook.

They followed the sound of the men's voices. The second they entered the study, three tall men in black tuxedos enjoying an aperitif, turned in the women's direction. All conversation ceased.

Pere smiled at Hallie. "When my beautiful wife was alive, her entrance in a room made everyone stare. Vincent and Max are two very fortunate men. Even Beauregard thinks so," he added as the dog ran circles around them.

"Thank you," she murmured. Her legs would hardly hold her up because of the look in her husband's eyes. He reached for her.

"Whether you're in a white blouse and skirt, or this fantastic creation, you take my breath," he whispered into her hair. "I'm more in love with you now than ever. I didn't think that was possible."

She melted against him. "I hope you'll still be saying that when you're Pere's age."

He released her long enough to cup her flushed cheeks in his hands. His dark handsome face radiated love. "Some things you just know. Our love was meant to be forever, mon amour."

She nodded. "Yes, my darling." Oblivious to everything else, she threw her arms around his neck and kissed him long and hard.

"What's going on in here?"

At the sound of a stern male voice, it was like déjà vu. Hallie wrenched her lips from her husband's and whirled around.

"Paul!" she cried in delight, unaware until this instant that the others had left the room.

He'd come in the study with a girl Hallie hadn't seen before. The lovely looking brunette had to be someone he'd met in Bordeaux. She seemed a little shy, a nice trait in Hallie's opinion.

"Papa? Hallie? Before the party starts, I'd like you to meet Brigitte Rambeau. We met in chemistry class."

The whole time introductions were being made, his date gazed at him with starry eyes.

Paul looked happy, expectant. She sensed he had something to tell them. Vincent sensed it, too. His hand suddenly tightened around her waist. But before Paul could say anything else, Monique came in the study with her latest boyfriend, Bernard. Hallie and Vincent had met him in Bordeaux.

Monique left him long enough to run to her father and kiss his cheek. "Don't you think Paul's news is exciting?"

Vincent brought Hallie even closer. "What news would that be?"

Paul's expression grew serious. "I've made my decision. I'm going into medicine, Papa. This fall I'll be starting my premed classes."

Hallie could just imagine the happiness those words brought her husband. Plus the added relief that Paul wasn't getting married yet. She also knew Vincent had to be experiencing joy that Paul had truly put the past behind him and was looking forward to a wonderful future.

Her husband let go of her long enough to give his son a bear hug. "You couldn't have given me better news, *mon fils*."

Monique came around to Hallie's side. "I've got some of my own," she whispered, but Vincent heard her.

"Ah, *oui?*"

"*Oui*, Papa." She beamed up at her father. "In September I'm beginning my business classes so that one day I can help you run the company."

As he embraced his daughter, his moist eyes found Hallie's. She had an idea Vincent was remembering the traumatic events that followed those nightmarish moments in his apartment over two years ago. No one could have predicted this outcome.

"Attention tout le monde!" Etvige called from the doorway. "Luc and Suzette are here looking for you two."

"We're coming."

The twins and their dates left the room, but Vincent pulled Hallie back in his arms.

"The night I drove Monique to the hospital to see Paul, she told me you were perfect, that if I would get to know you, I would think you were, too.

"She was right, Hallie. You *are* perfect." He crushed her against him. "I don't know what I'd do without you."

"I was just telling Gaby the same thing about you."

"Then hold on to me and never let me go," he cried emotionally.

"Never."

But she'd already made that promise in her heart the day she'd caught the train for St. Genes. She couldn't get back to him fast enough, back to this heavenly spot of earth and the man who'd been destined all along to be her future.

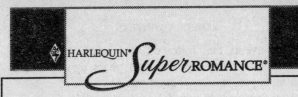

If this is your first visit to the friendly ranching town located in the Texas Hill Country, get ready to meet some unforgettable people. If you've been here before, you'll recognize old friends... and make some new ones.

Home to Texas
by Bethany Campbell
(Harlequin Superromance #1181)
On sale January 2004

Tara Hastings and her young son have moved to Crystal Creek to get a fresh start. Tara is excited about renovating an old ranch, but she needs some help. She hires Grady McKinney, a man with wanderlust in his blood, and she gets more than she bargained for when he befriends her son and steals her heart.

Available wherever Harlequin Superromance books are sold.

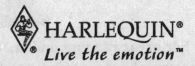

HARLEQUIN®
Live the emotion™

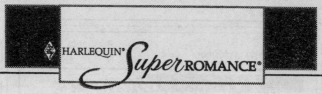

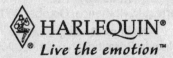

HARLEQUIN®

AMERICAN *Romance®*

proudly presents a captivating new
miniseries by bestselling author

Cathy Gillen Thacker

THE BRIDES OF HOLLY SPRINGS

Weddings are serious business in the picturesque town of
Holly Springs! The sumptuous Wedding Inn—the only place
to go for the splashiest nuptials in this neck of the woods—
is owned and operated by matriarch Helen Hart. This no-
nonsense Steel Magnolia has also single-handedly raised
five studly sons and one feisty daughter, so now all that's
left is whipping up weddings for her beloved offspring....

Don't miss the first four installments:

THE VIRGIN'S SECRET MARRIAGE
December 2003

THE SECRET WEDDING WISH
April 2004

THE SECRET SEDUCTION
June 2004

PLAIN JANE'S SECRET LIFE
August 2004

Available at your favorite retail outlet.

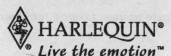
HARLEQUIN®
® *Live the emotion™*

Visit us at www.eHarlequin.com